The
Classroom

Also by
Alex R Price

Novels:
Anger to Rage
One More Thing
The Scholarship

Short Stories:
The Games People Play
Forgotten Dreams
Marbles
T.B.E.D.
The Newlyweds

The short stories and more information can be found at
alexrpriceauthor.com

The
Classroom

(INSPIRED BY ACTUAL EVENTS)

ALEX R PRICE

Squaretop Mountain Publishing, LLC
P.O. Box 593
Green River, WY 82935

ISBN - 13: 978-1-7332557-1-4

I dedicate this book to my mom for all that she had to put up with during my rebellious era.

Acknowledgments

I want to give a big thank you to Angela and Tammy. They have been two amazing beta readers that I have found since my literary journey began. I love their comments and insights to help bring about a great story.

I want to give a huge shout-out to my editor, Tracy. Her positive notes and striking red ink butchered my ego and rebuilt this novel into something extraordinary.

Lastly, I would like to thank the one person who is my biggest fan, though I have to keep her grounded by continually saying that she is biased just to get her to give me some constructive criticism. Thank you, Miss Kay.

The Classroom

Chapter 1

Sarah stood at the bottom of the hill. Fresh mud had covered her sweats when she slid to a stop in the miniature lake that had developed overnight. She looked back up the hill to see Drill Hawkins disappear into the mangled foliage from the previous night's destructive storm.

An eerie quiet engulfed her. The air seemed to vibrate, yet there wasn't a sound to be heard. She felt the vibration still, and confusion lingered in her mind until she made an attempt to move again. When it increased with her movement, she realized that it was her sore muscles playing tricks on her tired mind.

The uneasy feeling in the silent empty enclosure continued to eat at Sarah's sanity. The shock of the storm had muted the prattle from the unrelenting songbirds. They also must be gathering their wits and sorting through destruction from the storm's wake. The calm, quiet air left her feeling lost and alone as if she had just stepped onto a new world.

In a way, she had. Thoughts of monsters on an alien planet or Satan or some other dark creature hiding in an unseen crevasse surged forward to her conscious mind. The only thing lacking was ominous music preceding a horde of brain-sucking demons who would crash through the seven-foot security fence and end the pain and loneliness.

Large gates at the end of the enclosure sported a heavy chain and a titanium padlock. The heavy whitewashed two-by-six paneled fence was raggedly decorated with tree foliage from the savage winds that ripped through the area the night before. A small open gate to the side offered the only path to anywhere. Stepping over a fallen tree branch and out of the pond, Sarah made her way to the corridor leading out of the zip line landing zone.

The fence continued through a narrow passageway to a single door at the end of the run. To Sarah's right hung a plaque with the first of the seven core values that were beaten into her brain over the past two months. "Loyalty," she said out loud, breaking the silence that had engulfed her. Nodding her head, she agreed that this is what she must do. She could easily scale the fence, but she figured that if there were cameras where she came from, there were sure to be cameras here.

She paused by the sign that read Honor. Running her fingers over the wood grain, she thought about the sacrifice that Gloria had made for her. She thought about Gloria's three boys, whom she had never met. They wouldn't be able to see their mother outside of prison for the next ten years. They wouldn't get to go on vacations, sit around the dining table, cook a meal together or laugh at each other's absurd jokes. The freedom to vote or own a gun was a condition of nonfelonious acts and was of little importance compared to the freedom of being with friends and loved ones.

Glancing at the rest of the signs—Respect, Duty, Integrity, Personal Courage and Selfless Service—Sarah felt them deep inside. They were now infused in her brain, her stomach, her limbs and every cell of her body. She felt these core values all the way to her bones. She knew them and wanted them, but she had no idea how to use them. She felt like she had been given a finely crafted set of tools, but she had no idea for what or how they were used. She knew them to be necessary and now vital to her existence but couldn't think how they might be used in everyday life.

Looking back at the landing zone where branches mixed with sand and water, she realized that she had descended down a one-way path. It was as strong a symbol as any that there was no turning back. She had to go forward. She had committed herself to see the program through.

It was odd to her that in such a short time, she had come to see the world in a new and different light, and doing something for herself felt strange. She felt that if she did anything for herself, she would be reprimanded and shamed. She would be viewed as a selfish woman using anything that society had to offer for self-improvement as a tool for gloating. That is what she saw at every step she took. Each step now was a step for her and not for Gloria. In a way, she felt like she had fulfilled her life's mission and there was no need for her to move forward. Now she felt like a leaf lying in a stagnant pond, waiting to erode back into the earth.

Over the last few days, she had done everything for Gloria. She hadn't thought of anything else. She had done the bare minimum for herself: arranging her locker properly, shining her shoes, folding her laundry according to the drills' expectations. She had even skipped taking a shower when the drills were preoccupied with another task. In doing all that, she had managed to get a few more boulders to the top of the hill and eventually graduated phase one by completing Gloria's debt to the program. She didn't care if she graduated—she only wanted to clear Gloria's name, and she had done it with only minutes to spare. She had paid her debt to prove that Gloria had what it took to move on to the final phase.

Since the rules allowed Sarah to contribute charity work, she had been able to take on Gloria's punishment, finish paying the debt to the academy and clear her name to graduate even though she was facing the next ten years in prison. The prison that Gloria was sent to didn't count any time served at the academy toward shortening her stay with them. It was a flat ten-year maximum sentence that no judge could alter, according to the signed contracts between Gloria, the judicial system and the academy. That maximum sentence was the biggest incentive for each student to push forward and not fail.

Mirrored glass confronted Sarah when she reached the door to the phase two facilities. She looked at her disheveled hair still caked with mud from the night before. Someone had cleaned her up a bit after she had passed out from the night's exertion. A large bruise adorned her left cheek. The swelling had crept up to her eye, threatening to swell it closed. Through the narrow slit of her eye she saw the dried blood that caked her lower lip. She pushed at it with her tongue, causing it to split open again, and the crimson liquid oozed from the new opening. "Hell warmed over," she whispered to herself.

The numbness from her duty to Gloria had given way to the exhilarating adrenaline from the zip line, both of which had kept her pain at bay. Now she felt every bit of the pain. Every nerve screamed a severe complaint to her brain. The harness still draped around her frame felt like lead pulling her down toward a cold wet grave. Her muscles sagged from fatigue, threatening to never defy gravity again.

With great effort she lifted her hand to the stainless steel door handle. The button atop the handle wouldn't push down. She tried again. It still wouldn't push down. Tears crept into the corners of her eyes—she couldn't decipher if she was too weak or if it was God lashing out at her for all the cruel things that she had done. She lifted her other hand to assist, but the door wouldn't unlatch.

Panic ensnared her mind at yet another obstacle—this one so simple that she should have been able to overcome it. She should be able to push a simple button down to open a door. Sarah felt herself ready to collapse. Her legs wobbled, giving her a last-minute warning that gravity would soon win and pull her down to the cold wet earth.

A soft click vibrated through the door, followed by a gentle nudge pushing against her hands. Sarah stumbled back, barely moving fast enough to keep her legs under her. A soft voice caught her by surprise. "I'm so sorry. We keep this door locked unless we know someone is coming down." Perfectly groomed auburn hair framed the fair-skinned woman's face and her green eyes. She wore a custom-tailored suit that fit her well and demanded that people take her seriously. "I didn't know you were coming down. We had heard that the flag was still up at midnight. Many assumed that you didn't make it. I assumed so also. I'm sorry."

The name tag on her suit said Rebecca—Supply Clerk. She was a little shorter than Sarah and was just a bit thicker than a twig. She moved with confidence and stepped past Sarah to hold the door open for her.

"What do I do now?" Sarah stood stunned. Her brain had shut down. She couldn't even comprehend the purpose of an open door. She was too tired to think and wished for a simple command that she would gladly follow, even if she were directed to step into the pits of hell.

"Go inside. I know it's a beautiful morning, but you look frightful. The nurse's station is on your left. You'll go there first. Later, you'll come see me. My name's Rebecca. I'm in charge of supply. I'll get you your bedding, books and starter scrubs."

"What color are they?"

"Orange, of course."

Sarah's stomach knotted. Her face turned pale. She felt she would lose her lunch on the spot if she had any to lose. She couldn't remember the last time that she ate. She knew she had but couldn't think of when. Thinking nauseated her to the point that she was fighting off dizziness that would end with her in a pile on the floor. It took all her concentration just to stay upright.

"I'm sorry. It was a poorly timed joke. The scrubs are green, like the green grass of spring. It represents a fresh start. You look horrible. C'mon, let's get you inside." Rebecca held an arm out to usher her inside. Taking uneasy steps, Sarah made her way through the door and turned left into the open door of the nurse's office. Rebecca walked with her to help her find her way.

Anna turned from addressing the box of random drug test samples when she heard the conversation from behind her. Startled at seeing the large welt that threatened to swell Sarah's eye shut, and the obvious weakness and pain Sarah exhibited with every step, she rushed forward to assist and guide Sarah to an examining room. "Oh my god. You look horrible."

"Seems to be a popular opinion today," Sarah smarted.

"You made it. I knew you had it in you. I heard it took a bit to get you to color inside the lines," Anna said. She looked her up and down, doing a quick appraisal of the extent of her injuries, then patted the edge of the examining table. "Hop up here."

Chapter II

Two hours later, Sarah shuffled down the tile hallway. A shower and a clean set of scrubs left her feeling less than amazing but better than she had in the last several days. The ibuprofen that she was given did little to take the edge off her sore muscles and pain. She tried to put the blazing annoyance out of her mind and focus on what her next instructions were, but her body hurt more than she could remember—definitely more than it had after the beatings she had received from boyfriends.

She found herself asking for the instructions over again as her brain refused to focus on what was in front of her. Her mind could scarcely remember more than the previous few seconds that had passed. The numbness she felt left her in a vegetative state as she shuffled down the hall following Rebecca. Sarah tried to listen as Rebecca explained the layout of the complex.

"We have three residence wings. Each new class takes the section left by the graduating class. You will remain with your class in the same wing for most of your duration here. After you've completed all your classes here, you'll start your senior project."

"Senior project?"

"Yes. When you've finished all your classwork, you can choose one of any number of projects. You can become a drill and mentor a new student, even though we all mentor students. That's one of our jobs."

Sarah nodded her acknowledgment and tried to focus on the information, retaining all that she could. She noticed the hallways were decorated in photos of students and their achievements. One class stood in front of the elevated walkway that Fern had fallen off of due to her refusal to follow Sarah's directions. Sarah had given the correct directions, but Fern feared that Sarah would exact revenge and tried to counter what she thought were bad directions.

Sarah paused a moment at a familiar face in a photo. She leaned closer to verify what she thought she saw. In the caption below were the names of the students left to right. Jamika Hawkins stood in the second row and second from the left. She wore the same scowl yesterday as she did in the photo. The class of twenty-five wore mile-wide grins except for her. It looked like she was ready to rip someone's head off.

"Did she ever smile?" Sarah asked.

"Who?"

"Drill Hawkins."

"Sometimes if someone cracks a really good joke. Most of the time she is one hundred percent business. Once she's assigned something, she won't budge until it's done."

Sarah nodded, remembering the permanent scowl Drill Hawkins had just the day before. It seemed that she was trying to begrudge Sarah of any sense of accomplishment. She remembered the story she had heard about Jamika and the night her life changed. Sarah felt a pang of sadness for the woman and a longing to take her pain away. She knew what it was like to lose a child. She knew the anger and sadness that resided deep within her—the forever emotional torture that would continue to eat at her soul until she found a way to move on while honoring the life that could have been.

The gnawing pain Sarah felt was only temporarily subdued when her mind was distracted. Whether it was drugs, anger or drills, she threw anything up on that wall to distract herself from facing that demon and the failure that it represented to her. It was like she had to keep a constant twenty-four-hour watch going or it would sneak back in to claw at her heart at any time. It was easy to build a wall of anger. Sarah understood this and dove into that cycle repeatedly. It was hard to tear it back down knowing she'd be left vulnerable to those who could hurt her. The fear of being hurt again, of feeling that dreadful pain, of losing her mind to madness sent her on the offensive, lashing out at anything that might drag her into that dismal misery.

Sarah thought about Drill Witcom and her three sons that she wouldn't get to see for the next decade. How her sons would miss out on so much parental advice and, coming from Gloria, it would be golden advice. Her mind became a blur of emotions that mixed in with the exhaustion that kept them from being sorted and dealt with. She could recognize that they were there, waiting for the exhaustion to dissipate before making their way back to torment her again. She didn't want to feel. She didn't want to think. She just wanted to sleep—for a day, or a month, or a year, maybe forever. Instead, she followed Rebecca down a side hall.

The entrance to that hall had the remaining effects of its former prison bars minus the sliding steel door. The heavy floor and ceiling plates anchored the remaining high-strength steel bars. They had once been painted a dark gray color; now each bar had its own bright color of green or blue or purple. The varying rainbow of colors brightened the would-be dismal corridor.

Stopping at a steel door with a small shatterproof window, Rebecca peered in before opening the door. Entering slowly, Rebecca poked her head around the door. "Dean Vickery, am I interrupting?"

"No. No. Come in."

"I have your last student."

"Good. Bring her in."

Rebecca opened the door further and led Sarah into the room. Gasps erupted from her class. Whispered prayers and a general sigh of relief spread throughout the room.

"Twelve!" Faith leaped from her chair and wrapped her arms around Sarah before remembering the rule. Faith stepped back and set a hand on Sarah's shoulder, giving it a firm squeeze and a gentle shake. Sarah didn't know what to think. Her mind was numb from exhaustion. She reciprocated the hand on the shoulder with a gentle shake of her own.

In phase one, they were strictly prohibited from showing any type of affection. In phase two, Sarah learned that a hand on the shoulder at arm's length was the only kind of contact allowed and for no longer than two seconds. Sarah didn't feel that she deserved any affection because of what she had cost so many people. She had cost her classmates days of extra boulder hauling and cost a saint ten years in hell.

"Congratulations on your induction into our school," Dean Vickery said. "Help her find a seat if you would, please, Faith."

"Yes, sir." Faith quickly led her around toward an empty chair in the second row from the door. Lisa, Harley and Helen gave her shoulder or arm a squeeze as she passed by their desks. Faith pulled out the chair from the rectangular table.

10

Faireuza sat in the adjacent chair with an approving grin, ecstatic that their entire team made it to phase two.

"Thank you, Rebecca," Dean Vickery said. "Now Sarah, welcome. I was just telling the class about attitude and how it can affect the path you want to travel in life. Over the past few days your class was given a tour of the facility and instructions of what is expected during their time here. I'm sure your team will fill you in and help you get up to speed.

"It's not going to be easy, but I have faith that you will be happier, and your confidence will be better in a couple days. Faith has faith too. Right, Miss Faith? Dean Vickery gave Faith a staredown, coaxing her into the conversation to reassure her teammate.

"Whatever she needs help with, I'm here to help her, except math. I'm not good at math." Faith turned to Sarah. "Don't ask me about math. I'll probably tell you that two plus two is seven."

"Then why did you sign up for this business school?" Dean Vickery eyed her.

Faith looked up at the dean. "So I can get better at it. My mama always said to confront your fears, then master them, but that doesn't mean that I need to teach someone how to do math, unless they want to learn how to do it wrong."

"I like your answer, Miss Faith," Dean Vickery said. "Sometimes your attitude can become critical for you, the ones you love and even people you don't know."

"I don't understand," Ulyssa Vence said. "How can my attitude affect someone I don't know?"

"Let's take an example," Dean Vickery said, looking straight at Sarah. Sarah cringed. She knew that somehow she would be made an example of and ducked her eyes down to her hands, hoping to be forgotten about. "You might have seen a cartoon where the boss yells at the husband and gives him a bad day. The husband goes home and yells at his wife. She is not having a good day now. Their child asks for a snack and gets yelled at by his mom. The boy gets frustrated, then walks outside and kicks the dog. What did the dog do to get kicked?"

"That's a horrible story, sir." Faith was incredulous that anyone could or would hurt an animal.

"Faith, I'm sorry, but you have to face the reality that some people are not as ardent as you when it comes to the health and welfare of our four-legged friends. Some people are absolute saints, but most of us are in between, doing our best to make it through each day we wake up to."

Faith shrank back in her seat, reluctantly admitting that Dean Vickery was right as she remembered the incident at the soup kitchen. Jensen had zoned out and was about to take a knife to her attacker when Sarah wrapped her in a bear hug and carried her away. In an effort to escape, Jensen's attacker charged out the door and attempted to kick Roman, the former police dog, who twisted around and caught the man by the ankle, causing him to fall as the rest of the small pack acted to detain the man.

"Yes, sir," Faith said.

Dean Vickery, seeing that Faith was deflated, addressed her directly. "I have no doubt that you're going to do wonderful things with our four-legged friends. You can't tell people what to do or how to do it without having shown them what is possible. You have to teach the most obstinate animal that there is a better and more enjoyable life. That's when people will listen and start following your lead."

Sarah felt that Dean Vickery might have been directing part of that statement to her. She had, in the school's history, been the most obstinate person to graduate phase one of the program, aside from Gloria, who had to be the rock that Sarah broke herself against.

"Now the wave reverses," Dean Vickery said, continuing his story. "The boy gets in trouble by the mom. The mom complains to the husband. The husband is upset about the extra veterinarian bill and his work suffers due to his now increased stress level. All because the boss's wife became ill and caused the boss to be less than ideal and thinking irrationally in that moment.

"The point is that you can view everything as a cycle. Let's say that subject A decides to go downtown and randomly break into one shop or another. Now the shop owners are concerned and put pressure on the city council to hire extra patrol officers. The extra patrols keep the city safer. When the city is safer, the citizens want the city council to justify the extra expense of having more personnel on the force. The council trims the police budget and they reduce their staff back to the original number.

"Subject A's attitude cost the city tens of thousands of dollars, all because they wanted something that they didn't want to obtain by traditional means."

"Sir. I think most, if not all of us, have the right attitude for moving forward," Faireuza said.

"I believe that you do. This was a story about the cycle of attitude that if not changed, it will repeat."

"Repeat? What do you mean?" Helen asked. "It was a single incident."

"One single incident can create huge consequences. Most of you are too young to remember 9/11. We are currently in the guarding stage. Just like the example of the city guarding against the thief."

"So, do you think that the increased security at the airports will ever stop?" Faireuza asked.

"Yes. If something changes in society. Like the city example, there will be many factors that contribute to the decision to fund or defund the TSA." Dean Vickery looked across the class. He was pleased that they all seemed earnestly attentive. "It boils down to supply and demand."

"But isn't that a business term?" Faireuza asked, fully wanting to get the most out of this experience.

"Supply and demand can be levied against pretty much anything—from animals foraging for food in Africa to the rent increase in Salem because of this facility you chose to attend."

"What do you mean? Salem is over twenty miles away," Harley chimed in.

"Salem is one place that many of our facility's supplies come from. We buy from the vendors there. We hire personnel and teachers. We hire our security personnel from there and from other surrounding communities. The people who work here and there benefit from the academy by the flow of revenue that we generate."

"Don't we do a lot ourselves?" Faireuza asked.

"Yes, but we can't do everything. We can't make the computers that we depend on. We don't have a dairy to produce the milk products that we use in the kitchen. We are a small part of a very big picture. Where there is a transaction, there is commerce, and when there is commerce, life as we know it flourishes."

"So, because of the money going back and forth from this facility, we support other businesses in Salem?" Faireuza asked.

"You got it."

"So, what do we do for the community? How do we make money to support all this?" Stacey asked, waving a hand at the surrounding building.

"We control several businesses. We have a restaurant. We export produce grown by our students. We have a mechanic shop where our students learn how to repair vehicles. We have a pet adoption, training and grooming facility. We have initiated a test-run contract to train police dogs."

Faith sat forward, intent on hearing every detail. "How can I get started in training police dogs? I want to teach them how to sniff out drugs and tackle the bad guy."

"It's not that kind of police dog, Faith," Dean Vickery said, dashing her exultant expectations. "We'll be training them for use in the airports to detect contraband fruit and other food or substances. We have a few beagles that we will train and an expert handler who will help."

"When can I start?" Faith asked.

"After your first set of classes. In about three to four weeks," Dean Vickery said.

Faith started coming apart at the seams at the prospect of working with animals so soon. To train a working dog was the most tantalizing thing she could think to do. She wanted to start working with animals at that moment.

Dean Vickery looked at his watch. "Our time is up for today. What class do you have next?"

"Miss Gearda. Group counseling," Faireuza volunteered.

"That's right across the hall. Easy commute. Are there any last questions?"

"Yes, sir," Brenda Anskton said. Dean Vickery paused to allow Brenda to continue. "Do you teach any other classes?" she asked with a slight breathy voice.

"Just this one." Dean Vickery caught the intent of the question, as it had arisen with nearly every class. He found that women who had been away from male counterparts for extended amounts of time tended to develop a particular withdrawal that they would fervently seek to remedy with any person sporting the Y chromosome. "I will expect all of you to conduct yourselves professionally. This is still an incarceration, and you can just as easily be sent back to prison from here as you could from phase one. Any foot out of alignment, and you will get very comfortable with orange jumpsuits and locked doors." Dean Vickery gave a hard stare at Brenda. "This is a business school, and I expect all of you to conduct yourselves in a businesslike, professional manner, twenty-four hours a day. This is a fast-paced system. It is not for lazy people. If you slack off for even one moment, it could earn you more idle time than you want.

"We provide a quality education in an unconventional way. You'll receive four years of study in two to three years. We have professors that were handpicked to help you learn all the materials necessary to graduate with a degree. We have partnered with companies around the US, Canada, China and Mexico to come talk to you about foreign trade and what they expect when conducting business abroad. We have experienced managers come in to teach you how to lead people and not be a dictator on a throne."

Brenda humbled her enthusiasm and cowered in her seat from embarrassment. Coming from the highly physical and emotionally demanding phase one, her mind had now relaxed with her body and allowed her suppressed sexual frustrations to surface. She should have kept her eye on the overall goal and her mind attentive to her situation.

"You'll be graded with a pass or fail," Dean Vickery continued. "If you fail a class, you will be given one more chance to complete it. If you don't pass it a second time, then you are out. Some students who fail a class will wait awhile before attempting it again. This way they can study their problem areas in their off hours, then retake the class.

"After each class you will write a professionally addressed letter to the instructor thanking them for the knowledge you received, expressing the areas where you struggled and providing a possible solution that would have made it easier for you."

The class sat in silence for a moment, absorbing the strict expectations. Samantha raised her hand. Dean Vickery nodded in her direction. "Sir, you mean that we get to grade the teachers?"

"Yes. Feedback is crucial for any business. Whatever you do in the future will require feedback. That feedback may be a review of your product or service, or it may come in the form of returning customers or lack of returning customers. You won't be returning customers here. You only get this one scholarship. That's why we have you write a letter to your instructor while the class is still fresh in your mind."

Several heads nodded as the information rolled out across the classroom, but Sarah didn't nod. She was still digesting the total change in atmosphere, attitude and a glint of a possibility that this school was authentic, while contending with ultrafatigue and pain. Her original plan had been shattered by someone who had the purest heart she could ever imagine. One who had sacrificed herself for Sarah's chance at freedom—not from society or the judicial system, but from herself. It was a freedom that allowed her to feel and understand the basic rights she had as a human: the right to breathe and be alive, the right to think and make decisions, the right to feel emotions. With that freedom, she felt she could forgive herself of the guilt she carried about not being a good mother. She also felt the expanse of the universe open up and reveal the endless possibilities that were available right there at her fingertips. She felt wondrous freedom to do anything, except she didn't know what she wanted to do.

This new freedom also scared her. She thought it was like walking into a concrete jungle where she wouldn't know friend from foe. Instead of exploring all the new opportunities that

Dean Vickery was mapping out for the class, Sarah distracted herself by picking at the corner of a bandage on her hand. The energy to process all the information was more than she could handle at the moment, so she retreated back into the shy little girl she had once been, closed her bubble tightly around herself and focused on the corner of the bandage that peeled up with each flick of her finger.

Before her immersion in this program, she had filtered all her feelings through the empty anger that consumed her, blaming one person or the other for her problems. She hadn't realized that her problem was actually herself. It took a real mom to make her sit at the table and eat her vegetables, and in this case face the imaginary demons of her past and the demons masquerading as saints and disguised as parents. She thought of Gloria and how she could never pay back the debt she owed. There was no getting out of this contract. It was a mandatory ten years for Gloria, and not a day of previous time served was counted.

Her purpose for driving on was done. She had succeeded in completing Gloria's punishment. She had paid Gloria's debt so her name wouldn't tarnish the walls of the academy as a failure. Gloria could graduate and move on with her life. Though ten years was a long time to wait for that day. Sarah was done. There was nothing else she could do to help Gloria. She had nothing left, nothing to work toward; only an empty existence lay before her.

She felt empty again, but not like before. Her emptiness from before had stemmed from the lack of knowledge and the lack of a spark to her life. Now she had the beginnings of an understanding, and she had felt a spark of something wonderful, even if it was for only a brief time. But Sarah had completed that reason to keep driving on, to put one foot in front of the other. Now she had no reason to continue. She had finished her life's goal. Now there was nothing.

Too exhausted to think, she didn't bother to try and comprehend what Dean Vickery was talking about. In a zombified daze, she followed the others as they filed out of one classroom and straight into the next.

Chapter III

Days ticked by as Sarah learned the basics of her new routine. After receiving supplies for her bunk, she was shown how to make her bunk and arrange her belongings. Her scrubs were hung in a dorm room style closet with a locking door.

The pace of the schedule was rigorous but not as demanding as the boot camp's. This was more of a mental challenge than a physical one. Sarah didn't see any of the blue drill fatigues, though she did see a few of the drills dressed in custom-fit business suits. Some wore black, some wore blue, but they all wore their suits with their heads held high and proud of what they had accomplished.

Sarah found herself heading toward supply, seeking a pair of shoes. She had gotten a notice on her schedule to report to supply after the morning physical training. She shuffled down the hall, as the strap on her Crocs had broken and the shoe kept sliding off her foot, making a normal stride impossible. She had been about to ask for a replacement when she saw the order come through for her standard-issue shoes.

She rounded the corner and saw Rebecca waving her arms about frantically. The woman wasn't talking, yet the man watching her was grinning from ear to ear. He let out a hoarse laugh, like he had an extreme case of laryngitis. Sarah cautiously approached the two, curious to see what was happening.

The man wore a parcel delivery uniform that matched his dark skin. He gripped a hand truck in one hand and held a digital scanner in the other. His bald head had a glistening shine that reflected the overhead lights. After dropping the scanner into a clip on his belt, he flailed his hands about in a fashion similar to Rebecca's.

Sarah stepped just close enough to be noticed but not close enough to disturb the conversation. She recognized the flailing hand movements as sign language. Rebecca and the delivery man were engaged in an in-depth conversation that she had no way of deciphering. She stood quietly waiting for her turn to speak with Rebecca and admired the crafty waving of the hands. She wondered in amazement as their hands flew from one gesture to the next. Rebecca laughed and the delivery driver grinned as each completed their sentence.

"Excuse me, sir."

The all-too-familiar voice rang through Sarah's skull— instant alarm raced through her veins and adrenaline snapped her feet together with her fists at her sides. Sarah looked at the woman striding past her. Her hair wasn't pulled up into a bun; instead it hung down to just above her shoulders, still a little damp from a recent shower. The mute delivery driver moved aside when she stepped up next to him.

Jamika Hawkins set her bundle of fatigues on the counter. "Miss Rebecca, I need to turn these in."

"Of course, Miss Jamika." Rebecca addressed her by her first name, as was the custom once the students graduated from phase one. "Are you all done?"

"Yes, ma'am. I get my walking papers this afternoon."

"That's so exciting." Rebecca slid the blue fatigues to the side and pulled a receipt book from under the counter. "Where are you going from here?"

Jamika gave a sigh. "My grandmother lives just outside of Pittsburgh. I'm going to stay with her for the next year."

"Oh, that's wonderful."

"It's not like I have anywhere else to go, and she could use some help. She's losing her vision, but she was always good to me when I was growing up. It will be good that I can help her out."

"What about staying with other family?"

"They don't qualify. Too many ties to the gang members in Chicago."

"I see. Are you driving or flying?"

"Flying. I don't have a car."

The delivery driver tapped Jamika on the shoulder. Jamika turned to him, her face contorted into a scowl that made the man take a step back. He composed himself, and with a flash of his hands he began signing. Jamika threw her arms up, ready to defend herself.

"Wait!" Rebecca called out, fearing that Jamika might assault the delivery driver.

"What?" Jamika flashed a glance at Rebecca, then back at her supposed attacker.

"He is introducing himself to you," Rebecca explained.

"What? How? Why?" Jamika said, still keeping her guard up.

"His name is Landon. He just wants to say hello."

Jamika relaxed a bit but still carried a full-face scowl and kept her muscles tense. After seeing that he wasn't a threat, Jamika relaxed her face to indifference. She accepted his hand and acknowledged his greeting with just a nod of her head. Then she turned to Rebecca, grabbed the receipt, spun on her heels and walked back down the hallway.

Sarah had been invisible throughout the whole scene. She was grateful for the lack of acknowledgment through the tense confrontation. Landon began signing again. Rebecca signed back, adding words to her explanation. "No. She's not angry at you. She's angry at her past," Rebecca said. "She's a good person."

Landon flipped his hands around some more.

"You wish she would be staying here? Why?"

Landon signed again.

"Oh. I see," Rebecca said with a slight flush to her cheeks. "I will ask her. Will I see you tomorrow then?"

Landon nodded and waved goodbye, then started out the door, pushing the hand truck ahead of him with a package under his arm. Rebecca turned her attention to Sarah, who stood meekly in the corner, almost out of sight.

"Yes, Miss Sarah. What can I help you with?"

"Miss Rebecca, I was told that my shoes came in."

"Sarah Menendez, right?"

The skin shivered up her back at the sound of her father's name. It didn't seem bad before, but now it did. It had suddenly become the worst name she could think to give anyone. "Yes, Miss Rebecca," she finally muttered.

"Yes, they are here," Rebecca said, and turned to fetch the box.

"What was that all about?" Sarah lifted the shoes out of the box to examine them.

"Landon?" Rebecca looked toward the now vacant entry. "I really don't know."

"Oh. It seemed to me that he might like her."

"I think he does, but she's leaving. I don't think that she'll be back. Not many come back, except for the annual picnic. Jamika might not even come back for that."

"I heard about some of her past. I lost a child too."

"Oh. I'm sorry."

"It was a long time ago." Sarah pulled some of the now useless tissue and cardboard out of the box and slid it across the counter to Rebecca.

Rebecca accepted the wrappings and put them in their appropriate recycling bins. "If there's any place that can help, it's right here."

"I know. They've already helped more than I thought possible." Sarah traced the design lines on her shoes and tried not to think.

"That's wonderful. Do you know what area of business you want to pursue?"

"No."

"Is there anything that interests you?"

"Not really. I'm still trying to find my feet. I just want to rest for a minute and catch my breath. You know what I mean?" Sarah lifted the shoes out of the box and slid the box across to Rebecca.

"I know. The transition from the other side to here is huge, but you can't hesitate for long. You'll get left behind and get reclassed or sent back."

"Thank you for the heads-up and the shoes."

Rebecca gently unfolded the shoe box, then folded it once over so it would lay flat in the cardboard bin. "You're welcome. Let me know if you need anything else."

"I will. Thank you again." Sarah turned to leave, then stopped suddenly. She turned back to Rebecca. "How often does Landon come here for deliveries?"

"Usually twice a week. Sometimes more often."

Sarah nodded and returned to her class, thinking about the hostility Jamika exhibited toward Landon.

Chapter IV

"You're going down, Miss Cat," Shandel said, stabbing the challenge at her classmate.

"In your dreams, witch woman!" Catrina bellowed back.

Sarah mashed her back up against the wall to stay out of the way as Catrina muscled her heavy frame through the line of students waiting to get their lunch. She felt like the shy little girl afraid to speak her mind. In her junior high years, her obesity was constantly ridiculed, so trying to look small was impossible. Now it was almost as if she were pulled back into her twelve-year-old body, dodging one way or the other to stay out of the crosshairs of the prim, trim and proper.

The hostility between the two women echoed through the dining hall as Faireuza and Faith shrank against the wall next to Sarah, each holding their own trays of food. A shared look of bewilderment settled on each of their faces. This type of aggression seemed foreign, as it should obviously have been against the academy's rules.

Shandel muscled her way back in line and started scooping more eggs atop her plate. "Sorry for the intrusion, ladies, but I've got to take that woman down."

The woman she'd stepped in front of smiled and shook her head, apparently at ease and used to seeing this type of antics from the senior classwomen. After the tension had passed, Sarah hesitated a long moment before disengaging herself from the wall to search for a seat among her classmates. The environment was still new to her, and she wanted to succeed in the program, but the intimidation of the environment was overwhelming. She proceeded slowly and was extra careful where she stepped then finally settling in to a seat.

"What class do you have next?" The commanding voice was startling. Sarah instinctively snapped her body to attention and her eyes to the source of the voice. Drill Hooks stood before her, looking down at her plate of food.

"Drill Hooks."

"It's just Miss Kathy now."

"Miss Kathy. I have an algebra class," Sarah said, looking up from her plate as she placed her hands on her lap.

"Come see me in the commons area when you're finished. I want to talk with you."

"Yes, Miss Kathy."

"Great. I'll see you there." Kathy Hooks nodded her head and turned toward the door, arranging some papers in the crook of her arm.

****

"I've seen your scores, Miss Sarah. You don't need that class," Kathy said, evaluating Sarah and the rest of the small group. "I want to recruit you to my prelaw class."

"I thought you would be graduating," Sarah said.

"I'm retaking a couple upper level accounting classes here."

"You didn't pass them?" Sarah fidgeted with her hands as the embedded anxiety from Kathy's former role lingered within Sarah, causing her to second guess if she was doing the right thing.

"I passed them. I asked to retake them since I barely passed them. I'm retaking them to really learn the material. Since I'll be here for another trimester, Dean Vickery asked if I could teach a prelaw class."

"Trimesters. Right. I forgot that school is year-round," Evelynn Shoenstine said.

"We imitate the real world the best we can. Business is twenty-four, three-sixty," Kathy said.

"Twenty-four, three-sixty?" Evelynn asked.

"There are always a few days every year when you don't have to worry about the business," Kathy said.

"What days are those?" Evelynn asked.

"Days like Christmas, family reunions and SBA's annual picnic. Those days that you purposefully put it out of your mind to enjoy your time with family and friends," Kathy explained.

Nods and murmurs of understanding echoed from the small group.

"Since this is a business college, one of your beginning classes is Intro to Business Law. Learning how the law works is a necessity so you can avoid unnecessary pitfalls that cost employees jobs and cause embarrassment of running a poor business.

"I did exceptionally well in the class when I took it and all the following legal classes. After I'm finished here, I have a job as a paralegal in New Hampshire where I'll also finish up my law degree while working.

"Dean Vickery asked me to select several freshmen and bring him the list for his approval. I selected the eight of you as my first class. Dean Vickery approved you ladies because you did so well in your after-lunch class that you will be allowed to skip ahead to the next level." Kathy turned toward the other women assembled outside the cafeteria.

"Sue. You've worked with your father in his auto shop since you were little. You don't need a beginning autos class. You already know how to change oil and check your tires. Shaunteé, you already have a degree in mathematics—you don't need to go through precalc. All of you are really good with at least one of your subjects. That's why I was able to get you into this class and help you to graduate a little faster."

Kathy handed her syllabus out to each student. Sarah looked at the syllabus and the textbook it recommended, then skimmed the outline of what would be taught in the class. "What did I do that put me in this class?"

"In a minute, Sarah. The rest of you, go down and see Miss Rebecca. She has your new textbooks ready to go. I'll see you in room one-seventy-six in fifteen minutes."

"One-seventy-six? The syllabus says one-thirty-four," Sue observed.

"Yes, today we'll be in one-seventy-six because the building trades class is recarpeting that room. Tomorrow we'll be in one-thirty-four. Okay, ladies?"

"Yes, ma'am," Sue, Evelynn and a few others said.

Sarah continued to stare at the syllabus, looking for an answer as to why she was chosen. As the group headed out to see Rebecca in the supply room, Kathy stood and gathered her files. "Walk with me, please."

Sarah fell into step with her out of the learned behavior pounded into her during phase one. "I completely respect what you did for Gloria," Kathy said. "Everyone else does too."

"I still feel like I failed her."

"I understand how you feel. It's easy to feel that way. Phase one is about getting your mind right. It's about preparing yourself to learn. Helen hit the nail on the head when she disobeyed a direct order and went back in that lean-to, or rather, sod shelter. Although she and everyone else wanted to go in for warmth and a hot meal, she honestly wanted to completely transform who she is. From the start, she worked with the counselor to map out who she wanted to be and what she wanted to stand for."

"Wow. I never thought she would have that kind of drive."

"When you have a business, you have to study people. Do you know who the first person you need to study is?"

Sarah twisted her face, guessing at the answer. "The customer?"

"Yourself," Kathy said.

Sarah paused half a step, thinking about her outburst a few weeks prior when she blurted out that she didn't know what to do with her life.

Kathy continued, "To know who you are gives you deeper morals of what you are about. For instance, some teachers, after retirement, choose to keep teaching in one way or another. To them, it's not just a job; it's who they are at the core. If it weren't for needing money to put a roof over their heads, they would teach for free."

"So, I need to become a teacher?"

"No. What I'm saying is—"

Dean Vickery rounded the corner and nearly collided with Sarah and Kathy. "Oh, sorry ladies. Miss Kathy. Miss Sarah. I was just coming by to see you."

"You were, sir?"

"Yes. Of course. I like to introduce any new teacher to their first students here."

"Oh. That's right. I almost forgot," Kathy said.

"Where are you heading to?"

"I'm walking with Miss Sarah to supply to get her a textbook. Explaining a bit of why I asked her to join the class and a bit about what it entails."

"Great. I'll see you in room one-thirty-four then."

"Sir. One-thirty-four is being recarpeted. We'll be in room one-seventy-six today."

"Alright. I'll see you in a few minutes." Dean Vickery moved off down the hall, stopping in various rooms to chat with staff and students and tending to his well-oiled machine.

"Where was I?"

"You were telling me I don't have to be a teacher."

"Oh, right. You can be if you want. What I'm saying is that when you study yourself, you will see that you gravitate to something. This school pushes you to helping people, but it's up to you to decide in which way."

"What if I can't figure that out?"

"Then you pick something that you're okay with while you figure the rest out. In the meantime, Business Law is a requirement, and who knows, maybe it will spark something in you that will propel you forward."

Sarah nodded. "Yes, Miss Kathy."

"We'll see you in class." Kathy turned down a hallway and Sarah continued toward supply.

Chapter V

Sarah sat next to the fountain, watching the water cascade over the stones down to the small pond in the intimate flower garden. It had been two weeks since Drill Hawkins had shoved her off the platform. The knot on her head from hitting the rock after she sent the final boulder down the zip line was gone, but the scar was still evident and far from fading. The blisters on her feet had healed a while back, but their memory was still fresh.

She had exchanged the green scrubs for an approved school uniform that wasn't entirely comfortable, but wasn't the awful orange that she wore the first two months at the academy. It was the in-between status symbol of more than a grunt but less than a celebrity.

She watched the water flow over the rocks and breathed in the scent of the blooming flowers. A door opened to the atrium, and Sarah looked up to see her therapist walking toward her. Gearda was a very polite woman, but she never budged an inch when it came to her expectations of the students she counseled. Her thick auburn hair was neatly trimmed into a short bob. Her everyday casual clothes flowed breezily as she walked to the bench and sat down.

"Almost every student has been in here to sit and think." Gearda set her bag on the floor. "How's your bumps and bruises?"

"They're getting better."

"How are you feeling? Mentally, that is."

Sarah sat in silence for a moment. She hadn't given much thought to herself. She could only think of the woman who had saved her by sacrificing her own freedom.

"I feel like sh—" Sarah caught herself before uttering the prohibited word. "I feel horrible."

"In what way?"

"I failed the one person who cares for me."

"We all care for you."

Sarah raised her voice. "I've heard that so often that it's making me sick."

"You don't have to get loud."

Sarah calmed herself by clenching her fists, closing her eyes and taking deep breaths, then letting them out slowly as she relaxed her fists. "I'm not trying to be loud." Sarah sighed and calmed herself more. "It's nice that everyone cares, but I'm stuck on being a failure."

"Why do think you've failed?"

"Because I was stubborn and didn't tell anyone about my secret. I caused someone to go to prison. I took her away from her family."

"So, how did you make her go to prison?"

"I hit her and yelled at her."

"No. That's not what I'm asking. In the simplest of terms, what did you do?"

Sarah looked at the therapist, unsure of what she was asking.

Gearda continued. "All the students are here because they what?"

"They made a mistake?" Sarah asked.

"True, in a sense. When someone makes a mistake, it has an unwritten meaning of 'not intending the initial outcome.' Does that make sense?"

Sarah shook her head.

"Okay. Imagine that you're in preschool. Your friend next to you has a better finger painting than you do."

Sarah nodded.

"You want yours to be better, so you reach over and run your fingers through her painting. Did you make a mistake?"

"Yes?"

"You're guessing."

"No?"

"You're still guessing, but that's the correct answer."

"How's that correct?"

"Well, you succeeded in making your painting more attractive than hers. How can that be a mistake? Like when you hit your mother, you wanted her to feel pain like you did. I think you succeeded, but it wasn't the same kind of pain that you felt. Do you agree?"

Sarah nodded again. "Yes, ma'am."

"So, what did you do to your friend's finger painting?"

"I messed it up?" It finally clicked in Sarah's mind. She sat up straight, looking at Gearda. "Wow. I really messed up."

"Walk with me, please." Gearda picked up her bag and held an arm out, inviting Sarah to come along. "We're all stuck on this little blue planet. We can't go anywhere. As a country, we don't have any huge threats that would cause a national focus on a problem. So when the big picture is taken care of, you look at the small details.

"Our country is so diverse with different cultures, ideas and generations, that it's hard to be on the same page with any two people. Because we don't have a common enemy, we then turn to fighting ourselves and the ones we love."

Gearda swiped her badge over the sensor and Sarah opened the door for her. Walking into the administration section of the building, Sarah followed her therapist through the hallways. Gearda continued. "What we try to do here is a bit of the same pattern. We try to focus on the main issue, help correct the main problem, set you up with an alternate and hopefully better life and give you the education and tools to move forward and be as happy and successful as possible. Everyone has little issues and, for the most part, you as well as the other students are well equipped to handle them. Regardless, problems do come up, so we offer a support hotline for everyone who graduates here."

"Wow. You guys, I mean the academy, goes all out. What are some of the little issues that you've come across?"

"Believe it or not, we've had one student call in to ask how to turn on the dishwasher."

"Really?" Sarah's mind perked up at the oddity.

"She grew up in the projects and was from a very poor family. She went through our program and got a job with a decent salary at a Fortune 500 company. Shortly after, she started dating. Her boyfriend was very well off. She called to ask how to turn on his dishwasher because she hadn't seen so many buttons on an appliance before, and she didn't want to break it."

"Wow, and you helped her?"

"Some of our students operate the call center where they direct the call to someone or handle it themselves. A lot of the calls that come in are just for reassurance that someone is here to support them. We tell our students when they call to quickly outline why they are calling. If you need to vent, you say 'I need to vent.' This helps the operator understand that they need to listen and not give advice. If it is to learn how to run a dishwasher, the internet is readily available to find the information needed."

"Couldn't she just use the internet herself to find the information?"

"Sometimes, when someone gets frustrated, they don't see the answer that's right in front of them." Gearda stopped before a class picture with eleven students in the frame. She waved a hand to the photo hanging on the wall. "That's me. The second from the left in the back row. I was troubled like you were when I was young. I didn't have the childhood you did. Comparatively, I had a pretty normal childhood. Somehow, I developed a huge hatred toward my family. I was just angry all the time. I got into some trouble and was asked to volunteer for this pilot program.

"It was pretty simple back then. We went through boot camp much like you did and went to school at the university while having evening therapy classes." Gearda guided Sarah away from the picture and back down the hall toward the atrium. "My therapist back then kept asking me why I was angry. I really didn't have an answer. I was just angry. I really couldn't figure out why I was angry. They tried to put me on a medication, but all it did was make me fall asleep.

"No one really had a good explanation. I asked my therapist about it and he said that I might have to study and find out the answers on my own. So that's what I did. As I continued obsessively to find the answers in the college psychology classes, I somehow became fascinated and wanted to learn more. When I graduated, I paused to reflect on my journey and realized that the more I learned, the less angry I became. During my senior year, I don't recall ever being angry about anything.

"I came back to the academy to thank the dean for the opportunity to change, and he offered me a job. The academy pays me a fair wage. I enjoy a balanced life with family and friends outside the academy. I love what I do. I love seeing students going through their moments of understanding.

"Though it is run like a business, this school is like my extended family. Sometimes I feel like the aunt that everyone needs to explain the pros and cons of the decisions they face."

Sarah nodded, following Gearda back through the locked doors.

"Does everyone stay in contact with the school after they graduate?" Sarah asked.

"No. The majority do, but there are many who don't. We send holiday cards out every year. Some get sent back and we lose contact. Before they leave, we make sure they have the call number memorized. It's woven into our mission statement."

"Mission statement?"

"You know. What we say every morning to start our day and the little piece of paper posted on every door."

"Oh yeah. Right. I guess I never paid much attention to that," Sarah said.

"The school is run as a profitable business. There's a lot of hands-on training. The new students work as employees and work their way up to management. Every so often, a student will spin off a new business that will make the academy money. There aren't any CEOs to vote themselves a bonus. Everyone here works for a salary and sometimes they work for nothing."

"Work for nothing? Why would anyone work for nothing?"

"Sometimes they do it for the experience, sometimes they do it for the paycheck on the back end. A few who graduated here have set up nonprofit charities for causes that they held dear to themselves."

"I see."

"I wanted to bring you something." Gearda fished an envelope out of her bag and handed it to Sarah. "Do you remember signing a contract that gives us the permission to go through your mail?"

"No."

"It's one of the things we do to be prepared in case there happens to be bad news. We then can be ready to walk you through the situation and help you heal from the bad experience."

"Okay?" Sarah's guard went up. She didn't know what the mail might contain. From the counselor's words, she was expecting the worst, but she couldn't think of how bad anything else could get. Her childhood was horrendous. Her beginning adult years were little better, and her favorite person in the world was gone for the next ten years.

Sarah pulled the letter from the opened envelope. Her eyes flew over the words. Tears welled up in her eyes and she closed them tight. Her knees buckled, leaving gravity to pull her to the ground. Gearda jumped too late to catch her and her knees slammed into the carpet-covered concrete. Sarah sat back on her heels and hunched over the letter.

Gearda knelt next to her. "What are you feeling, Sarah?"

Sarah stayed hunched over her letter. A stream of tears flowed onto the parchment. A long moment passed as she held her breath—a breath that threatened to remain lost to her and leave her at the end of all her anguish. The rapture of air cascaded back into her lungs and she looked up at the counselor. "They believe me."

"Why do you feel that they wouldn't?"

Sarah lifted the paper and looked at it, crumpled and wet in her hand. "I was told my whole life that no one would believe me because my father was a police officer. His word was golden and mine was shit." Sarah looked up at the counselor after realizing that she had let a cuss word slip. She searched for a hint of understanding.

"It's hard to control the little things when the big things are much more demanding, but you know the rules."

"All debts must be paid," they said together in unison. The two women smiled together.

Sarah straightened. "I'll pay it." She picked herself up off the floor and brushed at her clothing to smooth out any wrinkles.

"Good. I'm glad to hear it. I talked to the county prosecutor in Trenton and he said that your father was arrested right after he was sworn in as a city councilman. The investigation is ongoing, and you will likely be called to go up and give a statement and a DNA sample. Your mom corroborated what she could of your story. The information was deemed credible, which led to a search warrant of your father's property and the collection of his DNA. A forensics specialist will be here this afternoon to take a sample from you."

"Okay. Doesn't the state already have a sample?"

"They do. This is just a double confirmation."

"I see. I can do that."

"When the time comes, we'll talk about what you will need to do and answer any question you have. In the meantime we need to get back to other business."

"Other business?"

"Remember, what is it that you are doing next?"

"What was that?"

"When you mess up, what do you do?"

Sarah stood staring with a blank face.

"We all mess things up in life. Sometimes they're permanent, sometimes they're not. Sometimes they only seem permanent," Gearda said.

Sarah looked Gearda in the face and caught the hint. Gloria's situation looked to be permanent and set in stone, but Sarah now felt that there was a chance. A chance to make things right. A chance to relieve her aching heart. Sarah thought about all the counseling sessions from boot camp. All the times of being reminded to take responsibility for her actions and to come up with solutions. "I can't go back and change it though." Sarah pleaded with Gearda, hoping for an answer.

"No. You can't. What other options are there?"

"Well, I can bust her out, but that would probably end badly."

"Yes. It probably would. Think on the legal side of the situation."

Sarah stewed for a moment before looking straight into Gearda's eyes. "I can get her a pardon." The therapist grinned at the young woman. "How do I do that?"

"Sounds like you have a direction." Gearda smiled, waiting for the student to soak in the wonderful feeling of knowing what her next purpose in life would be.

Sarah's gloomy mood lit up with the fire of a thousand suns. "Where do I start?"

"The library is always a good place."

"Gearda, thank you so much for your help. I have one more question."

"Sure. Ask away."

"Which way to the library?"

Chapter VI

"W ow, you do amazing work," Rebecca said, analyzing Joseanna's handiwork.

Sarah looked in the mirror at herself and the custom-tailored pantsuit. The midnight blue fabric framed her fair complexion. She paused and stared. Not a sound emitted through her lips as she stared at the woman in the mirror. A full minute ticked by before Joseanna sneezed, breaking the silence. Sarah stared into the mirror, searching for something that looked familiar. She searched for an angry face, a sour scrunch of eyebrows, a lazy comfortable sweatshirt, but she could find none of those things.

It was as if her brain had been transplanted into someone else's body. Her hair was pulled back into a neat bun instead of loosely draped about her shoulders, frizzy and in need of a brush. The heavy makeup she used to wear was gone, leaving clear, blemish-free skin due to the healthy food and lifestyle she had been forced into. Her eyes felt clear and unhindered by alcohol or drugs. She breathed easier and deeper than she had ever thought was possible. It had been months since she had had a cigarette. Now, she couldn't remember why she had liked them before. She now thought it a stupid impulse that drained a major part of her money.

"Sarah? Are you okay?" Rebecca said, stepping forward.

Sarah continued to stare at the mirror, still searching for something recognizable. With a mouse's whisper, she said, "I don't know who I am."

Rebecca rested a hand on Sarah's shoulder in reassurance and support. "You're Sarah," Rebecca said.

"No."

"No? Who do you see?"

"I don't know. I . . . I see . . ." Sarah searched the reflective glass for a hint of anything familiar. "Where am I?" Panic rose inside her. Her chest tightened as if it sensed an intense pressure building, and it contracted to stifle any release of energy that wasn't warranted. As her chest tensed, it caused the pressure inside to increase exponentially, threatening to choke her heart. The pounding of it increased until it reached her ears, stifling any sound trying to register with her brain. "I don't want to see this."

"Well, who do you want to see?" Rebecca asked.

Tears welled up. "Not this. I don't want to ever see this again." Sarah turned away from the mirror and flung the jacket off her shoulders. She half tossed, half handed it back to Joseanna and tore into the changing room. A minute later, she rushed back out, handed the blouse and slacks to the seamstress and bolted out the door.

****

"I thought I'd find you here." Kathy Hooks sat on the bench next to Sarah.

Sarah glanced over at the former drill. "How did you know?"

"A lot of women come to the atrium to get away from their problems. I did once myself."

Sarah looked over at Kathy, awaiting an explanation as she twisted her fingers together to help stifle her own anxiety.

"I had just graduated from phase one. I got to this side only to get news that my grandmother had passed away. She had Alzheimer's, so it wasn't so bad. The hard part was learning that it happened the day I arrived at the academy. The news was two months old when I got it.

"I hadn't been given a tour of the building yet. I took off running through the building, taking random corners until I came in here. I looked around, trying to catch my breath. Then I saw her."

"Saw who? Your grandma?"

"I don't know if it was her, but see that plant in the middle with the green and purple leaves?"

"Yes."

"I sat on the ground and talked to it for hours, thinking it was my grandmother. I know she had a beautiful plant like that before the disease claimed her mind.

"I told it all my secrets, all my feelings. I begged it for forgiveness and asked if it would help me heal and make it through this program."

Sarah nodded her head.

"When I finally looked up, Miss Gearda was sitting on the bench over there," Kathy said, pointing to the opposite side of the atrium. "She didn't say anything. She just escorted me back to the rest of my class and said, 'When you finish, I know you're going to make your grandma proud.' I've done my best ever since."

Again, Sarah nodded.

"I heard about you having a problem with your new suit. I wanted to find you and ask if there's anything I can help with."

"I don't understand."

"What don't you understand?"

"What is going on with me?

"What do you mean?"

"When I look at myself in the mirror, I . . ." Sarah took a deep breath and unclenched her fists. "I look like the people I grew up hating."

"Lawyers? Business suits?"

"Yes."

"Politicians?"

Sarah rolled her eyes and looked at Kathy with an obvious expression of disdain.

"I see." Kathy stood, then paced around the central fountain. "Miss Sarah, there are good people and bad people in all walks of life. There are good cops and bad cops. There are good gang members and bad gang members. There are good politicians and bad politicians. There are good teachers and bad teachers.

"Our job here is to teach you to be honest and respectable—first to yourself, then to others.

"Remember when you stole the blue team's flag?"

Sarah nodded.

"You took that opportunity for you and your team. You respected the other teams by playing by the rules. Except maybe for lending your shoe to Harley."

Sarah grinned at the mischievous assist. "I was expecting some harsh punishment for that." Sarah looked up at Kathy, anticipating an explanation.

"You gave her the shoe. There's no crime in that. She bolted from the chair, where she should have stayed, according to the doctor's orders."

"Didn't she get in trouble?"

"Well, it just happened that the doctor faxed a release before her feet hit the ground again. You can't get in trouble for following doctor's orders."

Sarah sighed with relief that her friend didn't get in trouble for that amazing stunt.

"In this school, we don't hold you back unless you're going in the wrong direction. As you've seen, many of our classes are self-paced. If you're a genius in math and you can bust out four classes in two semesters, we'll give you all the support you can stand. If you struggle with science, take it slow and methodical like the yellow team did while completing the obstacle course. But first, we have to identify the actual problem before we start working on a solution." Kathy waited until Sarah sat up a little straighter, indicating she was ready for the lesson. "When you look in the mirror, who do you see?"

"Someone I hate," Sarah said, resigning herself to the lecture and guidance.

"Why do you hate that person?"

"I hate her because she's never done anything right."

"There has to be something you've done right."

"No, there's not."

"Something recent, maybe? Involving boulders?"

"Yes. There is that. But I feel that it's a pittance compared to all the time I wasted getting to this point."

"Sometimes it takes an abrupt change in life to be able to look at yourself from a different perspective. Think of it this way—you just opened a door to a whole new side of Sarah. There will be many new things to explore and decisions to make. You will have to decide who and what you stand for."

"But, my life has been one screwed up thing after another," Sarah argued. "I can't do anything right."

Kathy sat on the bench next to Sarah. "You're learning to walk all over again. It's going to feel like you're falling down more than you're standing up, for a while anyway. Is there something that you want to do that is right?"

"Yes. I want to get Gloria a pardon."

"So, when you get an audience with the governor, how do you suppose you should look?"

"Not like this." Sarah looked down at her scrubs. Most of her class had already adopted the more formal business attire—a status allowed after they completed their first set of trimester classes. Sarah hesitated getting a suit, even though she had passed all the beginning classes for this reason. She felt completely out of place and uncomfortable in the business attire.

"Maybe an orange sweat suit?"

"Hell no," Sarah blurted out, forgetting the rule and punishment for the profanity. "Oh. I mean heck no."

"Gotcha," Kathy grinned.

Sarah's shoulders slumped even more than they had before.

Seeing she was close to another flood of tears, Kathy spoke up. "C'mon. I'll go with you. I said a prohibited word myself this morning. A little manual labor always helps clear your mind."

Sarah gave her a questioning look.

"I got a paper cut and dropped the f-bomb. C'mon, let's go pay our debts."

Kathy pulled Sarah to her feet and started her down the hallway.

"Miss Sarah?" A voice came from behind them, barely more than a whisper. "Drill Hooks? I mean Miss . . ."

Sarah and Kathy spun on their heels to find dark hair draped mostly over the right side of a young woman's face, hiding deep furrowing scars. Lloyd Temperance Kingsetter was half Native American and half European, but she seemed to take after her father with a lighter complexion while keeping her mother's dark Native hair.

She was a quiet and reserved young woman—she never spoke out and did everything she was asked to do. Sarah wondered if she was capable of stepping a foot out of line. She could always be found in the back corner, in the most out-of-the-way spot she could find. Sarah had heard some students refer to her as a chameleon because of her unique ability to blend into the background.

"Kathy. Miss Kathy. My name tag is right here. What can we help you with, Miss Temperance?"

Temperance's father had named her Lloyd Temperance after his father, Lloyd Temp. It was a name that plagued her her whole life—she wanted to change it but couldn't come up with the courage to ask it of her parents.

"I want to talk to the dean, but I don't want to do it alone. Will you stand with me?"

"Of course we will. As long as your intentions are good," Kathy said.

Temperance nodded and looked back at the floor.

"That is not an answer," Kathy's commanding drill voice trumpeted. "Stand up straight. Shoulders back. Head up. Now try it again with confidence and purpose."

Temperance did as she was told. "Miss Kathy, Miss Sarah, I would like very much if you both would stand with me when I talk to the dean."

Kathy looked at her pleading face. "Add a smile into the mix and you've got a deal."

Tension left Temperance's shoulders, and a meek smile spread lightly across her face.

****

The pressure on Temperance's shoulders became double now as she stood in front of Dean Vickery's desk. She glanced at him through the barely brushed tangle of hair that covered the right half of her face. The dean sat in his chair with his poker face that rarely showed its presence except when serious matters arose. Miss Gearda sat next to the window that overlooked the field where the students usually did their morning exercises. Her notebook and pen were poised comfortably in her lap, ready to scribble down any information relevant to helping Temperance succeed. Sarah and Kathy stood against the wall just inside the door, and when Temperance glanced backward at her classmates, Sarah gave her a supporting nod.

"I haven't been entirely truthful about why I'm here," Temperance began as her lower lip trembled. Dean Vickery waited patiently for her to continue. "I used to have a beautiful face. I won many beauty pageants growing up. I liked it for a long time. It was fun for a while. My parents divorced when I was twelve. My mom told me that my dad didn't want to see me anymore. He was too busy making money driving over the road. I believed her for many years.

"I was at a Miss Cornfield pageant in Kansas. I was sixteen at the time. I saw my father while I was on stage. I wanted to go see him, but my mother had thrown a restraining order on him and blocked him from watching me. He walked out the door and I never saw him again.

"In my paperwork it states that I cut up my face because of the stress of the pageants. That is true, but this is how it happened. A few months before I got in trouble and was offered a scholarship, I told my mother that I wasn't going to do the pageants anymore.

"We argued about it while she was cooking dinner. I told her that I wanted to find my father and drive over the road with him. She whipped around with the knife she was using to chop vegetables and made this cut right here," Temperance said, pointing to a deep scar under her right eye. "She said, 'Look what you did. You ruined a perfectly beautiful face. Your face was the only thing that was going to save your soul. Now you just as well have a face that matches who you truly are.' She shoved the knife at me and told me—" Temperance's voice caught in her throat and a tear rolled down her cheek.

When she hesitated, Sarah stepped forward, placing a comforting hand on her shoulder. "Keep going. You'll feel better afterwards. I promise." Sarah stepped back against the wall when Temperance nodded her head.

"She made me cut up my face . . ." Temperance straightened up and cleared her throat, grabbing any bit of confidence she could, and continued, "so that my face would match my soul.

"She threatened that if I didn't cut deep enough that she would cut three times as deep and three times as much. I did as she told me because I didn't want her to cut me worse. She locked me in a room until the cuts were healed. She blamed me for everything that went wrong. Being scarred up like that, I hid in the house. I didn't go outside. I didn't want anyone to see what I did to myself. I rejected all of my friends' phone calls. I don't know when or how it occurred to me, but I decided to leave. I knew that I was supposed to have twenty-four thousand dollars in my bank account from my pageant winnings. When I looked on my phone at my bank account, there was only fifty dollars left.

"I heard voices outside. I looked out to see a brand-new Mercedes convertible. Our neighbor was commenting on what a nice car it was. She told them that it was a gift from me to her for all the things she did for me.

"I let those words brew in me for several days. One night, I just took the car. I wanted to get away from her. I had to." Temperance paused to judge Dean Vickery's reaction and whether he would accept her reasoning for stealing the car.

"What happened next?" he asked.

"I got across the state line into Illinois, where I came across a herd of deer. I swerved through several as they bolted one way, then the other. I lost control and spun out, wrapping the car around a historic monument that the town was named after. Two deputies arrested me for reckless driving, a stolen vehicle and drugs in the car.

"The drug charges were dropped after my attorney found the body cam tapes showing the deputies planting evidence in the car."

Several seconds ticked by as Dean Vickery tapped a pencil on his desk, considering her story. "And?"

"Sir?"

"Temperance, what else do you want to say?"

"Nothing, sir. I just wanted to clear the air and my conscience. I'm sorry for my actions. I don't want anything to happen to my mother. I don't want to press charges or anything like that."

"And?"

"Nothing, sir. That's all that I wanted to say."

Dean Vickery evaluated his student, considering what she had said. "Nope. I'm not buying it."

"I told you everything," Temperance said, shocked that he would discount her story so quickly. "It is all true. I didn't lie to you. She did make me cut my face. I did swerve to miss the deer and I did avoid them. They all got away."

"Temperance, I've been a teacher, a principal, a superintendent and a father for well over twenty years. I can see a load of BS a mile away. You've been wanting to ask me something ever since you set foot on this side of the mountain. I can see it in your face every time you look at me. There is something you are dying to ask me. I've learned how to read people very well. It's my job to do that. Especially here. Sarah was a bit of a surprise. I didn't think she would have it in her until I saw her volunteer to carry boulders up the mountain for someone else."

Sarah's eyes went wide, looking intently at the dean.

"Early on, I learned that you can't judge a book by its cover. What I learned with Sarah is that even when you read the book over and over, you can still be surprised by an unexpected detail. I am exceedingly happy it was a good surprise."

Sarah tried to organize what she felt into a common category, but nothing seemed to fit. The only word she could put with how she felt was *verified*. It wasn't the hard DNA evidence to prove that she had been pregnant once. It was the fact that someone was watching and waiting for her to blossom into something beautiful.

"Now. Temperance, are you finally going to ask me what you've been dying to ask me since you got the green scrubs that you're still wearing?"

Temperance nodded and stared at the floor. "I want to drive a truck." The words came out in little more than a whisper.

Kathy cleared her throat very loudly and stomped a foot on the floor. Temperance snapped to attention.

"I want to drive a truck, sir."

"Why?"

Temperance hesitated a moment, preparing her reasoning. "When I was little, my father told me about all the wonderful things he saw. The sunrises on the east coast, the sunsets on the Pacific, the glacier lakes high in the Rocky Mountains and the waving grassland on the plains. I want to see what my father told me about."

"Temperance, you're only eighteen. It will be a few years before you can even get a commercial driver's license."

"I know, sir, but that's what I really want."

Dean Vickery stood and stared down at the pleading eyes. "No matter what, you're going to need knowledge of accounting, marketing, how supply and demand works in your field."

"Yes, sir."

"I can't fund a course for just one student."

"I know, sir."

"How determined are you to sit up in the driver's seat?"

Temperance took half a step forward and fixed Dean Vickery with a steady pair of eyes. "If I can't get that training here, then I'll get it when I get out. I mean, when I graduate."

"It's about time I got to see some fire in your eyes." Dean Vickery picked up his phone and pushed a button. "Susan, set a time two weeks from today. Lloyd Temperance Kingsetter needs an appointment with me to argue why we should start a truck driving school."

Temperance's eyes went wide, first from the surprise that the dean would consider an expensive truck driving school, then from the horror of having to face him and argue her point all over again.

"Miss Temperance," Dean Vickery said after hanging up the phone. "You have two weeks to compile all the information you can and present it to me and the academic board in support of the implementation of a CDL driving school. I want to see a full financial workup of the initial costs, maintenance and projected payback. I want to see the advantages and disadvantages that each student would face if they chose this career. I want a list of at least forty different specialized trucks that the students can operate. I want to know where the classroom should be set up. What materials you would need with budgets of a thousand, five thousand, twenty thousand and an unlimited budget."

"Unlimited? Sir?"

"Yes, unlimited. It's a good idea to know where that ultimate mark is. Evaluate the best system out there and the product it produces. Then to a lesser budget and the product it produces, and so on to every target budget that I specified."

Temperance stood dumbfounded, trying hard to interpret what she needed to do and how she needed to do it, all while trying to digest the possibility of her dream coming true.

"Talk to Mrs. Sunswick in marketing. Ask her about profitability analysis and how it might pertain to a driving school."

"Yes, sir."

"If you find that you need more time, talk to enrollment about dropping one of your electives. Got it?"

"Yes, sir."

"Anything else?"

"No, sir."

"You ladies may go." Temperance turned to leave but was stopped short by Dean Vickery. "Miss Temperance, I care about your past, but I care more about your future. If you don't want to press charges against your mother, that is up to you. I know telling someone your secret can feel like an immense burden lifted from your shoulders. I'm hoping that was the case this time."

"I do feel better, sir."

"What about others hearing your story?" Dean Vickery nodded to Kathy and Sarah.

"I never thought about that."

"I'll arrange a few minutes this afternoon to discuss this with her," Gearda volunteered.

"Okay. Kathy, Sarah, not a peep to anyone until you hear from Miss Gearda."

"Yes, sir," Sarah said as she straightened up. She knew all too well of hiding shameful secrets and that releasing those to an understanding ear could be the best medicine.

"It's not my secret to tell, sir," Kathy added.

"Very good."

No sooner had Kathy turned the door handle than the door burst open into her face. Jamika followed. She didn't stop to look at anyone, but kept going, right up to the edge of Dean Vickery's desk. Her face was twisted with pain, and a salt river of tears stained her cheeks.

Dean Vickery waved an urgent hand for the three students to leave.

Chapter VII

"How's the CDL training proposal going?" Sarah asked Temperance.

Temperance landed two fists to the face, clasped her hands around the neck and brought her knee hard and fast to the groin.

"Dang, girl. That dummy's gonna need a testicle extraction from his foam liver."

Temperance grinned. "I was trying for his lungs." She threw a block to the right arm and a knuckle to the tender flesh next to the bicep. "I'm having trouble getting enough students to make the class break even."

Sarah held the dummy firm while Temperance slammed blow after blow into the supposed attacker. "How many people have you talked to?"

"Over fifty students."

"There are over four hundred students here. You have to check with all of them."

"How do I do that?"

"Nearly everyone goes to church services on Sunday. See if you can make an announcement before the services start."

"I'll do th—"

A sharp, loud smack echoed through the self-defense training room. Sarah and Temperance looked around for the source of the noise. All other sound died out as the self-defense class came to a halt to watch Jamika slug repeatedly at a large bag hanging in the corner. With her back to the rest of the room, she hammered at the bag as if to rip it to shreds with her gloved hands.

Kathy Hooks, the self-defense instructor, quietly waved the two women over and ushered them out the door and toward the locker room.

****

"What's eating her?" Sarah asked as the class made their way out into the hall.

"Her grandma died," Helen offered. "She doesn't have any other family that she can stay with."

"What's she going to do?" Temperance asked.

"She's stuck here until she has an alternate plan," Helen said.

"What's she gonna do while she's here?" Sarah asked.

A loud crash followed by the angriest scream Sarah had ever heard radiated out into the hall. The class turned to see Jamika blur out of the training room and crash into Landon, who was simply carting a package down the hallway as Rebecca escorted him. In a protective move, Landon stepped into Jamika's path and accepted the full hit. Jamika shoved him up against the wall.

"You bastard!" Jamika screamed. "I fucking hate you." Jamika swung blow after blow into his middle, trying to pulverize anything that she could into a bloody pile. She let her anger course through her body, releasing the fury and

56

heartache wrapped up from the loss of her daughter and now her grandmother. Swinging wildly, she landed glancing blows and a few direct hits on Landon's body.

Landon stood like a tall oak tree after being shoved against the wall. Blow after blow pelted his body, with one glancing across his chin. Landon barely moved as Jamika flayed at him. Solid blows pulverized his ribs and arms. Landon tightened his muscles to defend against the assault.

Seeing an opening, Landon reached a big meaty arm out, grabbed a fistful of her shirt and jerked her to him. Jamika wasn't able to inflict the damage she wanted into the man, but that didn't slow her efforts—instead she redoubled them.

Sarah winced as she watched each blow connect viciously. She knew all too well how much damage those fists could do when they were filled with that kind of anger.

Jamika tried to push away, but the big arm held her tight. She again started pounding on his sides and back. A knee to the groin caused him to flinch, but he pulled her even tighter into his embrace.

The blows jabbed out in a never-ending cycle seeking to inflict damage, but the big arms held tight. There was nothing that she could do except surrender or wear herself into exhaustion.

Her cries of fury redoubled as she tried in earnest to damage any eardrum that could hear her. Her bruised and bleeding fists clutched at Landon's arms. Cries turned to muffled sobs as she buried her face into his shoulder.

Landon leaned down and kissed her forehead, doing what he could to comfort her. Jamika screamed from the depths of her soul and swung with all her might at the person holding her. The swing missed its target and connected violently with her jaw. Her arms dropped and her knees buckled, causing Landon to topple forward as he clung to her now limp body.

Stepping a size-twelve boot out and around the unconscious woman, he caught himself and prevented their collision with the floor.

"What happened?" Anna said as she came running from the infirmary.

"Jamika was working out some of her issues when she suddenly attacked Landon," Kathy said. "Landon held her tight to prevent her from hurting herself or him. Then she punched herself in the face and knocked herself out."

"Can you carry her to the infirmary?" Anna asked Landon.

Landon nodded, and with the most natural movement, he scooped up her legs and cradled her head against his shoulder, then followed Anna around the corner and out of sight.

"Wow. I was not expecting that," Helen said.

"Me either."

Sarah turned to see Rebecca standing next to her. She was startled at first, then realized that she had been the one that fetched the PA to come help with Jamika.

Rebecca continued, "If she likes you, you better plan on living longer than her."

The women stared down the allway, pondering the reason she had flung herself at an innocent man and the potential consequences for that type of action. The commotion had ended, and the few students who had witnessed it returned to class. The hallway fell empty again, save for Rebecca and the few women who were on their way to the locker room to get ready for their next class.

"Temperance. Your CDL book came in. I was writing a memo for you to stop by when Landon arrived. I needed to escort him to the kitchen and back for a package. Since you're right here, I don't have to finish the memo now."

"Awesome, Miss Rebecca. That's one more piece of the puzzle. Now, how am I going to get enough people enrolled to make it worthwhile? I also have to find someone who can teach the class."

"I'm sure you'll figure it out," Rebecca said.

"I hope so. I know that I've got a few years before I can drive a truck. I can memorize that book in a matter of months. What am I supposed to do with the rest of the three years?"

"I don't know," Sarah said. "But you better make a heck of an argument for it. Show him how bad you want it."

"Do you want to be one of the students?" Temperance asked.

"Miss Temperance, I would if I didn't already have a project that's consuming all my time," Sarah said.

"How's that going for you?" Temperance asked as they started moving slowly toward the locker rooms.

"It's about as frustrating as your project."

"How come?"

"I've got all of these classes, and no time to research how to get a governor's pardon."

"Can you ask one of the teachers or call an attorney?" Kathy offered.

The group of women stopped just outside the locker room door before Sarah asked, "Which one?"

"I don't know. Call any of them. They should at least be able to point you in the right direction."

"I'll try. What do you think will happen to Miss Jamika?"

"I don't know, but we better get changed and get to our next class. Miss Rebecca, I'll stop by and pick up that book after my next class. Thank you."

"You're going down, you short-haired huss," Catrina barked down the hallway.

"Bring it!" Shandel bellowed back, then ducked down a side hallway to her next class.

Sarah was annoyed at the animosity that Shandel and Catrina showed each other. She knew it wasn't serious, because she had seen them together working diligently on a few different projects. Yet she still didn't know what it was that they were aggravated at each other about.

Chapter VIII

"Are you ready for your presentation?" Sarah asked, picking up the easel and presentation charts.

"I hope so. Everything fits. I have sources for all the learning material. I have a maintenance budget for the equipment. I have two candidates for an instructor. I have a couple of example contracts showing that students would pay to reimburse the school for their education. I even got the local RC store to donate two remote control semitrucks with trailers that we can use to practice different scenarios with," Temperance said.

"Wow. Sounds like you went all out." Sarah held the door for her, then followed her down the hall toward the boardroom.

"I have everything except students."

"How many do you have?"

"Eleven, counting myself."

"How many do you need?"

"At least forty."

"Ouch. That's a lot."

"I know."

"Jamika. What the hell is wrong with you? It's like you're starting over at day one. That kind of behavior is unacceptable, and you know it." Dean Vickery's shouts could plainly be heard through the office door. Everyone within earshot stopped and turned toward the commotion. "I haven't lost my temper in over fifteen years, but somehow you triggered it."

"Just send me back to prison. I don't care anymore. I—"

"You should care. Because I can do a whole lot worse than send you back to prison. I can keep you here indefinitely. Now you will go find that young man, you will sit him down. You will buy him a coffee and you will apologize."

"I don't even know him."

"All the more reason that you need to do it. In fact, that is your next assignment. You won't be going anywhere or doing anything until you give him a sincere apology. You are to stand next to the supply counter until he shows up. Do you understand?"

"Yes. Sir," Jamika growled, and burst out of the office and stomped down the hallway.

Dean Vickery walked out into the hall and watched Jamika march off to supply. He turned his attention to Sarah. "How's your project coming along?"

"Slow, sir, but I'm making progress."

"Good. I'm glad to hear it. How about you, Miss Temperance?"

Temperance stood clutching her notes and files to her chest. She stood frozen, unsure of how to respond.

"Temperance is ready. Biting her bottom lip is a sign of total confidence," Sarah chided.

"Alright, ladies. See you in the meeting." Dean Vickery stepped past them and disappeared around the corner.

****

"How'd it go?" Harley asked, setting her tray on the table and pulling out a chair.

Temperance finished choking down a bite of food. "I did horrible."

"What happened?"

"I forgot Dean Vickery's name. I mixed up the names of the other board members. I tipped the easel over three times." Temperance took a breath. Helen, Sarah, Harley and Faireuza leaned in, listening for what happened next. "My voice squeaked. I dropped my note cards and got them all mixed around. Somehow, I managed to get most of the information out, even though it wasn't in the correct order. I was far from graceful. Not anything like you, Miss Harley. Especially when you flew across those ropes to save Miss Helen from falling. I knew I wouldn't be graceful like that, but I knew I had to finish. The only thing I did do well was make a 'neat and well-organized' handout. At least that's what they told me."

"Did they approve the class?" Teresa Campbell asked. She and two other young women crowded up to the table, eager to hear the answer. "Sorry I barged in on your presentation," Teresa continued. "We just graduated from phase one and heard about the class, and we wanted to get our names on the list. I hope we didn't get you in trouble."

"No. I think it actually helped. One of the special guests, Mary Kerjevec, said that she was happy to see the enthusiasm for that career."

"After we came down the zip line, I heard someone mention a truck driving class and a signup sheet. Miss Tabby, Miss Elisa and I rushed down to get our names on the list."

"Who all was there?" Helen asked.

"Dean Vickery, all six board members and six other guests. They introduced themselves, but I don't know what they do."

"Do you think they'll go for it, though?" Elisa asked eagerly.

"I don't see how we can. We just don't have enough students to make the numbers work."

"How many do we need?" Elisa asked.

"At least forty," Temperance said.

"Well, there goes that idea," Tabby grumbled.

"We're a small school. With a diverse occupation base. We won't be able to generate those numbers without sacrificing the numbers in other areas. That's not fair to those departments," Helen said.

"Ooh, look at you go, Miss CEO," Sarah said. "You sound like a business professional already."

The group chuckled, as they all had acquired much of the same mindset and vocabulary. A loud scrape rang out like a gunshot. The group looked up to see Jamika yank Landon into a chair. She stomped over to the cafeteria coffee dispenser, filled two cups and took them to the table. After returning to the counter to grab a handful of creamer and sugar packets, she walked back to the table and slammed them down.

****

Landon had no sooner set the incoming packages on the supply counter than Jamika grabbed him by the wrist and snapped "Come with me." Now he was sitting in front of a cup of coffee, watching the hands that had left multiple bruises on his sides a week before tear at the sugar packs and hastily dump the contents into his cup.

Jamika strode back to the serving counter, grabbed a pastry, a fork and two stir sticks, then plopped down in the chair opposite him and shoved the pastry across the table. Landon stared at the apple fritter, then at Jamika.

"I'm sorry," she snapped, and began roughly nudging the cup of coffee around in circles not caring if some of it spilled out onto the table or not.

Landon took a sip of coffee, then fished a notebook and pen from his pocket. Jamika sat and stared at her cup, waiting for him to finish scratching out a message. He turned the notebook around and slid it toward her.

"*I'm sorry that you feel so much pain,*" Jamika read, mumbling to herself, then sat back in her chair and folded her arms, waiting for the next remark.

Jamika stared at the floor, waiting for Landon to finish his cup of coffee so she could leave and be done with this assignment. Landon collected his notebook and took another sip of coffee. He added some creamer and looked at her. Scribbling down another message, he slid the paper across the table.

I know your heart hurts. If there is anything that I can do, please let me know, the note read. Jamika sat back in her chair again, unfazed by Landon's attempt at healing her spirit.

Landon withdrew his notepad, wrote out another message, and slid it in front of Jamika. *I want you to have this. My mother has collected these her whole life. I like this one the best.*

Jamika glanced at the second piece of paper being slid across the table. *January 11, 1960* was printed in the top left corner of the yellowed newspaper clipping. Four panels depicted the mini story of Charlie Brown and Linus pondering the future and happiness. Her jaw clenched tight; anger spread across Jamika's face. Landon's hopeful expression dropped when she didn't react as he would have thought. In a flash, Jamika snatched the paper from the table, tore it in half and crumpled it in her fist.

Landon's jaw dropped. A bit of the ebony color drained from his face. All movement in the room stopped; the entire cafeteria was watching the drama unfold.

"Jamika Hawkins." The booming voice cracked the charged air like a clap of thunder. It was the unmistakable tone of a father scolding his child, and it riveted everyone's attention on Dean Vickery. "I need to see you in my office immediately."

Jamika stood with a huff, dropped the crumpled comic strip on the table and stormed out of the cafeteria past Dean Vickery. Whispers gradually grew into the normal cafeteria chatter. The dean walked up to Landon, apologized for the display, then asked if he could keep the torn and crumpled comic strip. At Landon's nod, he flattened it carefully and tucked the cartoon inside a folder before shaking hands with the tall, silent man.

Dean Vickery turned his attention to Temperance, Sarah and the rest of the young women seated around the table. His mood brightened considerably. "Ladies. How's lunch?"

Chapter IX

Temperance bit her lip, anticipating the news that Dean Vickery was obviously there to deliver. A sturdy woman who had been standing in the doorway when Dean Vickery called Jamika's name walked up to stand next to him. The blue pants suit she wore looked unnatural on such a woman—she looked like she belonged in jeans and work boots. The yellow visitor tag was squared above her left breast pocket, and Temperance spied the top edge of her handout peeking out of a green folder that she carried.

Her hair was short, barely down to her collar, and mussed up with gel. The little makeup that she did wear looked out of place, like it didn't belong on her face. Her build seemed more suited to a bodyguard or someone who stacked bricks all day.

Although her appearance seemed ill-fitting, her demeanor was spot on. It was punctual and factual; she was someone who frowned on a watered-down version of the facts. The way she carried herself was very much businesslike.

"I'm Mary Kerjevec—no relation to the Shark Tank investor." Mary looked around the cafeteria. "Wow. It's changed a lot in a decade."

Sarah and the rest of the students stared slack-jawed at the visitor. "You were here before?" Helen asked.

"I was. I was in the second class here. Right, Dean Vickery?"

"No. You were in the third class. That was the first time that we took on a class of twenty-five students."

"Oh, that's right." Mary turned back to the mix of business suits and green scrubs eager to hear more of her story. "The academy had just bought this facility. I took the building trades classes, and one of our projects was to replace the damaged and outdated ventilation ducts. We had a class and a scope of work followed by a safety meeting, then we would work. If one of us came across a problem, Mr. Johnson would stop work and quiz us on how we would fix the problem. Then he'd show us how he would do it."

"Miss Mary, what'd you do to get offered a scholarship?" Elisa asked.

Mary looked at the woman with an expression that would snap a brick. "Isn't our focus here on what we can do in the future and not marveling at shortcomings of the past?"

Elisa shrank back and answered, "Yes, Miss Mary."

"We're here for your future, and to a lesser extent, ours."

"Miss Temperance, why do you want to drive a truck?" Dean Vickery asked.

"My dad told me about all the wonderful things he saw traveling across the US and Canada. I want to see what he saw."

"Did you consider all the bad parts of the job? All the paperwork, traffic, breakdowns and weather?" Mary inquired.

"Yes. Everything I've learned here so far has shown me that I'll have good and bad days, and I wouldn't know how great a good day is unless I also knew how horrible a day could be."

"How bad do you want to drive?" Dean Vickery asked.

"Sir. I'm gonna drive even if I have to teach myself."

"Now that's the best answer I've heard all week."

Temperance's anxiety grew in the short silence as she waited for Dean Vickery to continue.

"We've decided to put a class together. A trial run."

Grins spread around the table like a blossoming flower. "That's awesome," Temperance said.

"When do we start?" Elisa asked.

"I think we should have a class ready in about two months. We'll let those with the soonest out times sign up first."

Temperance's face dropped for a moment, then brightened. "Who's going to be our teacher?"

"Funny you asked," he said with a straight face. "You are."

"Me!" Temperance shot to her feet. "I don't know anything about driving. How can I teach a class when I don't know what or . . . or . . . or how to teach?"

"You'll learn. The three wardens who watched your presentation were impressed by your passion and determination to see that the project is implemented. They're going to watch your first set of students and see how well they do, while assessing their hireability. If all of them land driving jobs within the first thirty days after release from here, then the wardens will sign contracts for you to teach your class at their facilities."

"Sir. Class at their facilities?" Horror spread across her face at the mention of leaving this facility.

"Yes. We'll set up an improvised classroom here," Dean Vickery said.

"And when your students attain their CDLs, my company will sell the academy a box van trailer at a reasonable price,"

Mary added. "Midknight Transportation will lease out one of their old simulators with an option to buy. Bluesky Logistics will sell a fleet truck to the academy for some hands-on training. They'll also make a couple of their trucks and veteran drivers available to explain permits and to demonstrate loading and securing loads and oversize loads."

"What if I can't deliver? What if I fail somehow?"

"If the program fails, then I'll expect a forty-page report of how and why it failed," Dean Vickery said. "But you're not going to fail, are you?"

"No. Sir."

"Good, then I won't have to worry about reading a forty-page report."

"But sir. How can I teach the things that you can only learn through experience?"

"Trial and error. That is what the simulator is for. That is your first step in gaining experience. Your first class will help you learn. You'll be here for a couple years, so when you turn twenty-one, I'll expect a perfect score when you take your test."

"When you're released from the academy and have your license, you have a guaranteed position in my fleet," Mary added.

Temperance wanted to run screaming down the hallway at the better-than-expected news. She felt so giddy inside that she was afraid she would explode.

"We'll reduce your class load a little," Dean Vickery chimed in, "so you can prepare for this trial run. Our finance department can help you design the course, tests and evaluation questionnaires to help you improve your coursework."

Temperance stood stone-faced. She didn't know whether to be overjoyed at her dream presented to her or terrified that she was now leading a class with zero knowledge of the subject.

"Miss Temperance, you can breathe now," Dean Vickery said. Temperance blinked at her name, not realizing he was talking to her. "Look, you're going to be fine. As long as you strive for excellence, we'll back you up one hundred percent. We'll check on your progress in two weeks."

Dean Vickery and Mary bid their goodbyes to the group and left them to their meals.

****

If Dean Vickery had ever seen an angrier face, he couldn't recall when. The ridges across Jamika's brow furrowed; her eyes were unblinking, staring at the empty space right above the desk.

Dean Vickery appraised her for a moment. "Look. I know you lost your grandmother and that's a horrible experience. Now, I feel that I am forced to do something for the first time in the academy's history."

"Send me away. I don't care," Jamika said. "There's nobody else out there for me. So, send me back to prison."

"Oh, you're not going to get off that easy."

Jamika looked up at the dean. She hadn't thought that there was anything worse, let alone something that made hard time seem like a walk in the park. She knew that Dean Vickery didn't bluff, and she felt his eyes piercing her soul as if the devil's might. He appraised her with a devious smirk. Alarm bells blared inside her head, calling for her to recant her words and actions. She shoved them aside, determined to bull her way into a prison sentence.

"Just send me to prison. I'm not going to play your petty games. I'm not going to be your model student anymore. I'm not going to be your example. I'm not going to be anything to you or this damn academy."

"If that's what you want." Dean Vickery picked up the phone and dialed an extension. "Mrs. Thatcher, are the papers signed for Jamika Hawkins?" He paused on the phone, listening for a beat. "Okay. Good. Send a security detail down here for transport. Okay. Thank you."

Soon after the phone clicked back onto its cradle, the door opened. Two large male security officers entered, followed by a female officer and Gearda, who handed the papers over to the dean. He flipped through the pages, looking for all the appropriate signatures.

"You're acting like a three-year-old in need of a belt. Your actions were completely uncalled for and hurtful toward probably the only person who might want something to do with you."

Jamika sat stone-faced, praying for transport to show up and haul her out of this jail masquerading as a school.

"Do you have anything you want to say on your behalf?"

"Just send me away. Get me out of this dump that you think is so wonderful."

Dean Vickery stared at her for a long moment. His face drooped in resignation. He had tried everything he could think of to get through to her. The papers required his final signature. He sat in his chair , then picked up his pen and bent over the papers, dreading having to do this a third time.

Chapter X

Sarah resisted the urge to slam the phone back down on its cradle. She had been written up twice the week before for "abusing office equipment," as the paperwork had stated.

She was frustrated with the endless cyclical go-to shuffle of trying to chase down the right person. The process of trying to get an innocent person out of prison was exasperating. There were long lines of people all professing their innocence, compounded by the melee of proper procedure—technical glitches threatened to send her back to the start. The pace was gruelingly slow, with multiple redoes necessary for any one little typo.

The multitudes of people calling in to proclaim the unfairness of the judicial system and seeking corrections to their charges seemed to congest the process and cause a bottleneck, transforming average citizens into a preschool class of attention-seeking toddlers. Sarah felt that she was close to throwing her own tantrum at the slow process.

The academy had paired her with a local attorney, who passed her off to his paralegal. The paralegal was a dedicated employee who took her job seriously, but Sarah felt that the woman was condemning her for life because she was in a detention facility.

"We're closing for lunch in five minutes."

The voice jolted Sarah out of a daze. Her hand jerked and inadvertently pulled a few strands of her bleached hair from her scalp. The Hispanic roots were forcing out the remnants of a quickly fading era. She had derived them from her father along with his last name—a name she loathed and would discard as soon as she could. Shaking the hair from her hands, she looked up to see Karman, who had landed a job as the librarian of the legal library. She was the only one who seemed to be helpful and encouraging to Sarah. "Oh, okay. I'll wrap it up."

"Are you making any progress?" Karman asked.

"Little to none." Sarah started gathering her notes and closing the half dozen books she had pulled off the shelves. "It's like an uphill battle. As soon as I tell whoever it is that I talk to that I'm a convict, they hang up or politely find an excuse not to help."

"I know how you feel. What helps me break through some of the red tape is asking them how they are and being genuinely caring. Ask for small favors first, then bigger ones. Build a relationship with them first and always ask if you can do anything for them."

"Sounds like something Dean Vickery would say." Sarah stood up and pushed in her chair.

"He did. That's what he told me when I was having trouble connecting with people."

"What were you working on?"

"I'm interning through Davidson and Halls. At the time, they were representing a land acquisition where multiple parties were involved. Everything had to be down to the letter,

74

and the punctuation had to be precise. When I called someone, I had to identify who I was just like you did. When they hear 'intern,' they tune you out immediately. The receptionist seemed to get more respect than I did. I have an associate's in paralegal, but that means little to some people."

"What'd you do to get in trouble?"

"I don't want to talk about it. Best to let sleeping dogs lie. I'd rather look where I'm going instead of where I've been. Since we need to look where we're going, how about I buy you lunch?"

"Sounds good. I'm hungry and I could use a break. How much longer do you have here?"

"Ten to fourteen months." Karman fingered the keys that locked the door while she waited for Sarah.

"Do you have any job prospects, people ready to hire you on when you're finished here?" Sarah asked.

"I'm contracted to start working with Steinman, Hiltz and Katchman in Newark, New Jersey."

"You are? How does that work?" Sarah finished putting the heavy lawbooks back on the shelves, then walked past Karman and out the door.

Karman closed the door and locked it. She turned with Sarah and walked down the hallway. "I'll work for them two days a week while I go to school full time. After a few more months I might get bumped up to three days a week. Once I graduate there, I'll intern with them for twelve months, then move on to get my law degree. After that, another twelve months to finish my contract. How do you like studying law?"

"It's alright, I guess. Trying to get an audience with the governor is a pain in the backside. If you know what I mean," Sarah said.

"So, what's this woman's story? I've met her and we've done a few things together, but I don't know much about her," Karman asked.

"To me, she's the greatest person to walk the earth. She got me to really pay attention to who I am and what was going on in the world around me."

"One moment," Karman interrupted.

Sarah waited for Karman to turn in the key to administration and sign the register. "From what I understand, she tried to save her niece from being born in jail by claiming the drugs in the car were hers and not her sister's."

"So, she admitted to something she didn't do? Because she admitted to it, she doesn't get a chance to appeal to a higher court. She's SOL without a governor's pardon," Karman said factually.

"What about new evidence? If her sister says, 'Hey those are mine, she was covering for me so my baby wouldn't be born in prison,' and you get key people to believe her, then that would constitute new evidence."

"Possibly, but it would also be evidence against her for perjury," Karman added.

"So, she's in a catch twenty-two," Sarah grumbled.

"I wouldn't look at it like that. I would look at it as, which is the lesser of the two evils. I'm going to guess and say that perjury can carry a hefty sentence, but if you factor in the reason for the perjury, a judge would likely be lenient with her."

"How can you be sure?"

"You can't, really. The laws are the laws. It's basically the judge's job to select an appropriate sentence. So, the case would be argued for the reason she did it and the result of that action. They may also take into consideration that she has served a significant amount of time already."

Turning into the dining hall, Karman grabbed a tray and handed a second tray to Sarah. Sarah accepted it with thanks and stepped into line behind her.

A culinary student stood facing them, her notebook open on the counter. Dozens of tally marks scored the page. "Good day, ladies," she said with a fading hint of an Australian accent.

"Hello, miss," Sarah said.

"Good day, Miss Elizabeth. I mean Chef Elizabeth," Karman said.

"This weekend we are bringing in some snow crab. There is a limited amount; therefore we will have a drawing for the people who get to choose that entrée."

"Oh wow, that's a first." Karman's eyes lit up. "I can't remember the last time I had snow crab. Please sign me up."

"Sure thing, and what about you, Miss Sarah?"

"No thank you, I'll pass."

"How come?" Karman asked.

"I don't feel like I have much to celebrate."

"Why not?"

"I'd rather not talk about it—not now at least."

"Okay." Karman turned back to Elizabeth. "What else will you be serving?"

"These are my own recipes. We will be serving a chicken saltimbocca drizzled with a fruit sauce and served over rice. We have a beef stir-fry with our garden vegetables and fresh dinner roll. We have a couple vegan dishes available: kohlrabi baked with a variety of vegetables and herbs or a vegan spaghetti with my own vegetable-infused sauce. It is so good it might even convert a few steak enthusiasts. And finally, a lime-marinated salmon steak served in a Véronique sauce and garnished with a slice of lemon."

"Ooh. That sounds heavenly. So, what are the tally marks for?" Karman asked.

"We're trying to get an idea of what dish everyone would prefer so we can reserve those ingredients in the garden."

"Nice. Put me down for the chicken if I don't draw the snow crab. And put Sarah's name in too. I'll see if I can cheer her up. Help her see that she's worth a small reward every once in a while."

Elizabeth nodded and wrote down Sarah's name.

"So, you're graduating soon?" Karman asked.

"Yes. Culinary school anyway. This is like my senior project. I'm running the whole show. Everything's on me," Elizabeth said with worried zeal, tapping her pen in rhythm with her varying mood.

"You get to invite family, don't you?" asked Karman.

"Yes. My mom and baby brother are coming. I also invited Gordon Ramsay, but I haven't heard a response back."

"Oh. Wow. That's a tall order. You know that, right?"

"I know. I just wanted to tell him thank you for giving me a different and positive direction to go in my life and that I might be coming after his title very soon."

"Alright. That's the competitive spirit that the dean likes to see."

Elizabeth grinned.

"Good luck, but I already know that you'll present an amazing, delicious feast."

Sarah delivered her well wishes and followed Karman down the cafeteria line. She wished she could be as upbeat and positive as either Karman or Elizabeth, but the dread she felt for Gloria facing ten years in prison sucked any ounce of joy from her.

Chapter XI

The alarm clock chimed through the ceiling intercom. It was usually nature themed—birds chirping, a babbling brook—or instrumental music that morphed into a classic rock ballad or an up-tempo country hit. Sarah thought it entertaining that every time the babbling brook played, the morning rush to the toilet seemed a bit more urgent.

It was five thirty on Wednesday morning, almost halfway to the day of rest before the torturous routine would start over again. She craved Sunday's glorious extra hour of sleep like all of her classmates did. Marking another week off the calendar helped to reenergize her. Her graduation date was fluid as far as an actual date was concerned, but she knew that it would be within a few weeks of her completing all her classes and assignments. Graduation was still a long time away and she didn't have a clue what she would do afterward.

She had taken to running several miles every other day out of respect for Drill Hawkins and their time together during phase one. It was one thing that she wanted to maintain and something that she found an unexpected joy in. The wind in her face and the pounding of her feet in rhythm with her heart gave her the small euphoria of feeling alive. Now a far cry from who she had been, she was sure none of her old friends would recognize her.

Staring at the ceiling in the minutes before the five-forty-five alarm, Sarah sighed and reminded herself of the decisions that got her there—first, being ill-tempered toward her mother and society, and second, stepping up to accept responsibility for her actions. She felt Gloria would be disappointed in her if she saw her now: a flailing mess searching for the light switch in an endless night. *"How could Gloria be proud of me? I don't know what I'm doing. I don't know what direction to go. I don't even know if I'm worth the effort that so many people have put in to save me from a lifestyle I'm bound to go back to. What is there to keep me from going back?"* These thoughts consumed her brain, which was seeking reassurance that she was going the right direction.

Her clouded mind almost made her late for the 6 a.m. formation. She tied the laces on her shoes, grabbed her water bottle and bolted for the door, trying to make up the time she wasted contemplating her life's choices and whether they were still the right ones.

Running to the formation, she stepped in to the back just a few seconds before attention was called. The green sweats she wore showed her association with her graduating class. Some had already pledged to attend an annual reunion picnic the first few years after being released. Sarah knew how people tended to go their separate ways when there wasn't something forcing them to stay together, so she didn't hold out much hope that the pledge would be upheld.

Dean Vickery stood atop one of the small mounds in the field. Several mounds had been built across the exercise field, and the students rotated from one to another to allow the grass to recover from the abuse of the morning tradition.

Whenever he didn't have an appointment somewhere else, Dean Vickery started off the assembly. It was also a meeting where staff and students would be brought up to speed on general finances and any special awards that students had earned. It was a tradition adopted from the Chinese culture, where the stimulation of blood flow throughout the whole body increased the productivity of daily tasks and created an overall more pleasant work environment.

This morning, Sarah recognized Drill Hooks, Drill Smith and Drill Abernathy standing on the mound next to Dean Vickery. "Those who can attend," Dean Vickery started off, "are encouraged to stop in to the rec room to celebrate these wonderful students being sent off into the next chapter of their lives. They will be there later this afternoon as they have a few things they need to do, as well as a mountain of papers they need to sign before they go. This time they'll be flying over the inner gates and marching out the outer gates into the arms of their loved ones, and I hope I won't see them again until the annual reunion picnic. In fact, I had better not see them," Dean Vickery hazed in a playful manner.

After a quick reflection of how far they had come and where they were going in the future and a quick bit of advice, the three former drills resumed their spots in their now vacant class. The rest of their class, with the exception of Gloria and Jamika, had already moved on to better things.

Dean Vickery paced back and forth atop the mound. "Our graduates will be in the rec room most of the day. Please find time to stop in there to bid them farewell and good luck on the next leg of their journey.

"In other news, our produce section set a new record with total weight sold to the community." A cheer went up from the students and staff. "But Miss Stephanie crashed the van into a fence—now our automotive team is getting some good training on body repair."

"Yes, but I didn't hit the family of skunks crossing the road," Stephanie blurted out.

The assembly gave a chuckle while Dean Vickery stood atop the mound looking very much like a proud father. "True, very true. The dash cam confirmed that the family of skunks made it out unscathed, and we don't have to give the van a tomato bath.

"Where is Miss Temperance?" Dean Vickery asked.

Sarah looked forward, searching for Temperance amidst the sea of green sweat clothes. On the far left, a thin arm reached high, announcing her location.

"Over here, sir," Temperance said, barely loud enough for Dean Vickery to hear.

"Are you ready to start your first class tomorrow?"

"Yes, sir."

"Good to hear. Sorry that we couldn't get a mentor here for your first day, but we did find one. He should be here in about two weeks. He's kind of an ornery old cuss, but he's very qualified to help teach you and your class."

Sarah watched Temperance do her own little happy dance—what she could anyway, while standing in formation. Temperance was all teeth, standing in formation waiting for the exercise to begin. She had worked so hard putting the program together, and now it was happening—she had her very own class to teach, which was both scary and exhilarating. Sarah figured that becoming a teacher before becoming a student was the most asinine thing she had heard of, but Temperance's passion was deserving of that chance. She had worked hard for the opportunity to make the academy a better place, and now it had one more career path to offer future students.

They all deserved some good in their lives, something or someone to offer a chance to break out of their former molds. Whether their lives had been fractured during their childhood or early adult years, or they were led down the wrong roads or just allowed to be influenced by the wrong people, they all deserved something good. Something that would make what they were going through worth the pain and confusion. Something that would add value to who they were, happiness in their heart and a better understanding of what kind of people they were.

Most, if not all, the young women at the academy had some sort of past that had taught them to behave less than ideally by society's standards. Sarah was no different. She followed the example of her parents: take what you want until someone says no.

Sarah could plainly see all the excitement and growth that surrounded her, yet she didn't feel it. She didn't want to go back to the lifestyle she had before. Yet, she still didn't see what lay ahead for her. She felt like she was swimming in a giant void where nothing existed. No happiness. No sadness. No excitement and no pain, just a numb state of existence. She compared how she felt to one of her classmates who was diagnosed with bipolar disorder. While on medication, her classmate described much of the same feeling that Sarah felt now.

Gearda had told her it was depression and asked if she wanted something to help with that. Sarah agreed at first, but later in group therapy, Helen expressed that she would try anything first before going on medication, as she didn't want to be dependent on pills the rest of her life. Gearda said that step one was to recognize the depression. Step two was to know that it would come and go. Step three was to find something small to achieve, and her mood would soon start to turn.

Sarah tried it on one occasion, and it worked. After dwelling on her problem all day, she asked Karman if she could do something simple to help take her mind off her problem. Karman gave her a stack of books to replace after explaining the Dewey decimal system, then had her vacuum the library. After an hour of mindless chores, Sarah noted that she did feel better. The next day she found the answer that she sought, though later it turned out to be a dead end. But she now understood the concept and made a reminder note and posted it on her desk in her room.

"Don't forget that Miss Elizabeth will be turning our cafeteria into her own restaurant," Dean Vickery continued. "I know that my name is in for the snow crab drawing, but looking out across all your hungry faces, I can tell that my chances of drawing some snow crab are really slim.

"Miss Elizabeth, I know you're going to have a successful evening. You have your assembly crews ready for the transformation?"

"Yes, sir. They are ready to roll as soon as Saturday's lunch is finished."

"Sorry, Miss Kathy, Miss Susan and Miss Heather, you can't stay for the snow crab. We're kicking you outta here."

"That's alright, sir. I think we can manage. When she gets her own restaurant, we'll be her first customers," Kathy said, giving Susan and Heather fist bumps before looking over at Elizabeth. "And there better be some snow crab," she heckled.

"Alright, if you want snow crab, you better get your feet off the ground!" Dean Vickery yelled across the formation.

A cheer went up as feet started hammering the ground in place, beginning the morning routine.

Chapter XII

Jamika had lost count of how many laps she had made inside the tiny eight-by-eight-foot cell over the last several weeks. The door opened to the shower only three times a week, leaving her sticky with sweat for the days in between. Flimsy paper gowns were all she was allowed to have. She had to ring the buzzer any time she wanted to use the bathroom or brush her teeth. Even getting a drink of water was cause to ask permission.

She couldn't do anything but be angry. The first few days, she had stewed and beat against the padded walls. She screamed obscenities at Dean Vickery, the counselors and anyone else who crossed her mind. She screamed at the guards who kept her locked in the cage. She screamed at the unseen people who delivered her food and buzzed her into the bathroom.

After a week, her voice was hoarse, and her hands hurt from beating on the wall. She tried to behave, in an attempt to be let out, but they didn't respond. No one did. They just watched her from the camera in the ceiling. She flipped them the bird numerous times, trying to elicit a response. Any response would have been acceptable.

She tried urinating on the floor as opposed to asking to use the toilet. She was met at the door with a dose of pepper spray, followed ten minutes later by a four-person team who wore body armor and chemical masks and used a fire hose to wash down the tiny room, soaking the paper gown off her. After she had shivered in the corner for an hour, the shower door unlocked. Jamika trudged into the shower, admitting the small defeat and hoping to warm her body in the hot water. A puddle of combination bodywash and shampoo sat in the stainless steel tray welded solidly to the stainless steel walls.

Ripping what little remained of the paper gown off her body and discarding it on the floor, she pressed the button to start the shower. Several seconds of cold water sputtered out of the showerhead before it turned lukewarm, then hot. In two minutes, the water would be turned off. If she didn't have all the soap washed out of her hair and off her body by then, she would feel sticky for days until she was allowed to shower again.

Being locked in the shower, she had to wait until her room was cleaned and disinfected. Warm air blew down on her head, so she used that to help dry her hair. The towel they provided was too small to wrap around her body, so she folded it and placed it on the steel bench where she sat and waited.

A new paper gown awaited her atop the foam sleeping pad in her cell. She dressed in the gown, scooted the foam pad against the padded wall, then sat there stewing over everyone and everything that did her wrong.

Weeks had passed, yet Jamika's anger didn't soften. It simmered on a low heat, waiting to be unleashed. The dim light above never blinked—there was no way she could judge time. Even her meals came at irregular hours.

THE CLASSROOM

Waking from several hours of unusually restful sleep, Jamika sat staring at the empty space just a few feet in front of her. She sighed and glanced around the room. Nothing had changed. She stretched her arms above her head, looking at the black globe fifteen feet above. She contemplated flipping it off, but resisted the urge. Her gaze traveled to the door. Still shut. But the window was open.

Jamika jerked her head back to the window. The window wasn't open, but the padded cover had been slid to the side. Her heart dropped. She wouldn't be able to see out anyway. *"What's the point of a window if you can't see out?"* Jamika thought.

She was about to continue brooding about her predicament when she saw something in the bottom corner of the window. She had thought it was a shadow in the dim light, but the angle was wrong. Cautiously, she stepped to the door.

Taped to the outside of the thick acrylic window was a blank piece of paper, and taped to that paper was the *Peanuts* cartoon she had ripped and crumpled up. Written above it was a simple question. *Why would he want you to have this?*

Jamika stared at the question, then at the message in the cartoon. *"Outrageously happy."* Startled that she had said the words out loud, Jamika looked quickly around the room to see if anyone heard her. No one was there.

Suppressing her feelings guarded her from being hurt. It had become her coping mechanism for moving forward until she could reach her grandmother's house. Her grandmother would always smooth things over, but she was gone now, and Jamika had no one.

She looked back at the paper. *D.V.* was inked in the lower right corner. Dean Vickery had set this up. Anger creased her face. She fumed that he was still trying to manipulate her, trying to get into her mind.

"You trying to teach me a lesson?" Jamika yelled. "You trying to make me one of your little soldiers?" She faced the camera on the ceiling and gestured with her arms. "Why did you keep me here? Why didn't you ship me away to prison?"

A thump hammered on the window. Jamika spun and looked. A new piece of paper clung to the window. *Answer the question.*

"I'm not going to answer your goddamn question!" Jamika screamed.

The pad slid shut on the note and the cartoon. Then the lights went out. She stumbled around the room, beating on the wall until she tripped over her bed. Collapsing onto her bed, she fought to keep her defiance, hammering her fist into the pad over and over before drifting off to sleep.

****

A creak of squeaky iron woke her. Opening her eyes, Jamika could see that the dim light was on. A cold draft sent a shiver through her body. The door stood open. She had an eerie feeling that a monster was waiting for her to step out of her sanctuary to claim its next victim. Another shiver shook her body a little more violently this time.

Cautiously, she got up and peeked out the door. Dean Vickery sat in a chair and waved a hand, inviting her to join him in the outer room. The solitary confinement cell had an outer room constructed for this purpose. It was a practical as well as a psychological instrument to dissuade detainees from thinking they could escape through the double set of doors.

A thick, soft blanket hung over the vacant chair that was placed facing Dean Vickery, inviting Jamika into its warmth. She sat down and pulled the blanket around her shoulders and tucked it around her feet and legs.

"Why are you doing this? Why not just send me to prison?" Jamika asked.

"You already know the answer to that."

"I do?"

"Yes."

"How? How the hell am I supposed to know that? Quit being so damn cryptic, Harold."

Dean Vickery mentally flinched at hearing his first name. It was reserved for his wife and close family, while other close colleagues just called him Vick. He had been called many worse things before, but this one gave him pause. He respected Jamika, and that's what made this situation hard. He knew her well enough that giving up would be the worst thing he could do to her.

Dean Vickery gave her the briefest moment of consideration, then continued. "Ask yourself what you would do for your daughter."

"Everything."

"Wrong answer."

"What?" Jamika blasted, just about coming out of her chair, then thought better of it.

"Wrong answer?"

"How is it a wrong answer?" she said, remembering to keep control of her emotions.

"Would you rob a bank if she asked?"

"No. What kind of mom do you think I am?"

"See? You wouldn't do everything, just like you wouldn't have done her laundry when she got older."

Jamika stared at Dean Vickery, knowing that he was right, but not wanting to admit it.

"If someone held your daughter hostage and you didn't see any way to get her back safely by going through the authorities, what would you do?"

"Anything."

"See the difference?"

Jamika nodded. Dean Vickery poured a cup of coffee out of an old beat-up thermos and handed it to her. She accepted the cup and took a sip, savoring the warmth before settling back into her seat.

"This was my father's thermos. Whenever he had a lesson to teach or he needed to console me when I was struggling with a problem, he would grab a couple of tin cups and a thermos—hot chocolate when I was little and coffee when I was older—and we would sit on the back porch watching the fireflies and sort out what I needed to do.

"Sometimes I didn't think it helped, but when I look back, it was just what I needed one hundred percent of the time.

"Now. Please answer the question."

"Question?"

Dean Vickery glared at her over his cup of coffee.

"I don't know why he would want me to have that."

"Two words. What is it about?"

"My grandma showed me the same one. I think that's why I got so upset."

"It's okay to be upset. We just need to find an alternative way for you to deal with it."

"Yes, sir."

"What was your grandmother like?"

"I don't want to talk about it, sir."

"So, you want her to fade into oblivion so no one can remember her or know who she was as a person. Was she that horrible of a grandmother?"

A bit of fire reignited in Jamika's eyes. She sat up straight and looked at the dean. "No. She was a wonderful, caring person. She would do anything for you."

"Tell me something that she did, or that you and she did together."

"She caught me stealing candy when I was six."

Dean Vickery took a sip of coffee and waited patiently.

"I kept it in my pocket and looked at the floor, hoping no one would notice me. When we got to the checkout counter, she asked to see the manager. When he arrived, she asked if he could put all the groceries back for her because she couldn't afford them anymore.

"When he asked why, she told him that I had stolen a candy bar and that she had to save her money to pay for a lawyer.

"The manager looked down at me. I remember him as if he were a giant. I froze. I didn't know what to do. My grandmother then handed her keys to the manager. She told him to please take her house and car. She was always polite like that. She said that she would need more money so that the jail would be able to take care of me and that she knew it would cost a lot."

Dean Vickery listened intently, only turning the tin cup in his hand occasionally.

Jamika, silenced in thought, continued to stare at the floor, then continued. "I asked her where she would live. She told me that she knew where there was an old dirty mattress under a bridge. She told me she didn't know what she would have to eat.

"She turned to leave; I ran after her and caught her sleeve. I begged her not to go. She told me that even though I took the candy bar, she was responsible, and that she would have to pay for it because I was still little. She told me that when you take from someone else, it costs a lot more of everyone around you, especially the ones you love.

"I cried and turned back to the manager. I handed back the candy bar. I had squeezed it so tight that it was completely deformed and unsellable. I begged him to give grandma's house and car keys back. I begged him to let her go home where she would be happy.

"He gave me a really stern look and told me that if I stole anything again, he would come and take grandma's house and make me go to jail, where mean people lived.

"I did everything I could to help grandma after that. The money I made from lemonade stands, I put in her money box. She told me not to, but later I would sneak it in there. I didn't want her to be without a home.

"I was a good kid all through high school. Got good grades. The one time I went out after hours to a house party, I got pregnant with my daughter."

Jamika paused, not wanting to go on. The pain from the loss of her daughter still hadn't fully healed. Most of the time, she avoided the subject and thought she had dealt with it, until her grandmother had passed.

"Sounds like you really cared for her," Dean Vickery said, pulling her away from the pain of losing her daughter.

Jamika nodded.

"Did she point that comic strip out to you specifically?"

She nodded again.

"Did she say anything about it?"

Jamika nodded again. "She said that it was her favorite."

"What type of person was she? Was she moody and mean? Did she just feed and water you?"

Jamika smiled at the lighthearted joke. "She was happy. She had a different view of life than most people. She seemed to always be able to find the silver lining in anything. She was the type of person who could talk a salesman out of his commission and have him feel good about it."

"So, you knew her pretty well, then?"

Jamika nodded.

"So, if she were here now, what advice would she give you?"

"To pull my head out of my ass, but in much nicer terms."

"So, what is the message?"

Jamika thought it over.

"Two words?" Dean Vickery reminded her.

Jamika stood, keeping the blanket wrapped around her shoulders. She walked to the door and read the comic again. "*Do you ever think about the future, Linus?*" she began, reading the faded yellow parchment dated January 11th, 1960. She mouthed the words from the second and third panels. "*Outrageously happy,*" she finished.

A minute ticked by as the gears in her mind found the necessity to start turning again. She turned to the dean. "Future and happy?"

The dean nodded and gestured for her to continue.

"Why would he give me that? I've been a total bitch to him."

"Well, in the simplest introductory form, what is he asking? You have to ask yourself, if you couldn't speak, how would you communicate?"

"He can't talk?"

"No, Jamika. He can't."

Jamika looked at her bare feet on the tile floor. She suddenly looked at the dean. Realization flashed through her mind and reflected in her eyes.

"Good. I can see that you're starting to put all the pieces together. I'll leave you to your work. It seems that my job is done here." Dean Vickery stood to leave.

"Sir?" She waited for him to pause. "How do I talk to him?"

"Jamika, I'm sure he can read. Can you write?" He blasted the words at her as if it were obvious. "You can keep the blanket once I see a good letter of apology."

Jamika nodded in understanding. "Sir, can you please leave the comic up on the window?"

"I planned on it."

"And sir, how will I know when I'm done?"

"Well, I would say that that is up to you." Dean Vickery picked up his father's thermos and walked out the secondary door. Two guards entered and checked the articles for accountability and searched the padded room, then directed Jamika to go back inside. They locked the padded door but left the window visible with the comic taped to the outside of the glass.

Chapter XIII

Saturday was abuzz with excitement and anticipation. The drawing had been postponed because a water leak in a storage closet had soaked all the names in the ticket tumbler. The ink ran and many of the tickets were stuck together.

Sarah finished straightening the covers on her bed. Her language arts book and workbook were set on the corner of her desk, ready to go to study hall.

Monday through Friday was nose to the grindstone, with very little time to keep pace with the rest of the class. It wasn't a requirement to keep pace—the classes were designed to be self-paced—but instinctive pressure urged all the students to push themselves so they wouldn't get left behind.

"They should be announcing the names for the snow crab dinner soon," Helen said, poking her head over the top of Sarah and Helen's room partition.

"I know. It's going to be great. I know Miss Elizabeth can't wait to see how everyone reacts to her entrées. I heard she put a lot of effort and her own earned money into this." Sarah finished her bed, then turned to her clothes in her locker.

She wanted to earn an extra few hours to relax in the atrium. She loved hearing the birds chirp as they flew from branch to branch, arguing over territory.

She figured that she wouldn't draw the snow crab dinner and resigned herself to looking forward to the chicken. The morning announcements cued and rattled off a few standard updates to the earlier broadcast.

"Now, what everyone has been waiting for all week: the lucky people who get Chef Elizabeth's mouthwatering snow crab. First name out of the tumbler is Nancy Halbrick. Second name is Samantha Wick. Our third lucky student is . . . Oh. Well. This isn't a student at all. Mystery guest? Is that right, Dean Vickery?"

Sarah, Helen and several others froze, straining with all their senses to grasp why another student's name wasn't being called.

Dean Vickery's voice chimed in to the intercom. *"Ladies, we have a special guest coming to visit us. Everyone who attends has their name put in for the drawing. I hope our guest will be an inspiration to many of you. He has agreed to give a short speech and answer a few questions. Back to you, Miss Janet."*

"Ooh. Mystery guest. Alright. Thank you, Dean Vickery. Back to the drawing. The next name we have is Sarah Menendez," Janet said.

"You got one!" Helen's excitement exploded as if she had drawn one of the prestigious plates herself.

Sarah smiled, but she didn't know how she felt about it. She had resigned herself to the chicken dinner, so drawing a plate of the snow crab seemed phantasmic. She thought it was nice, but she wanted to maintain her focus on her upcoming study hall. She wanted to learn how to write with such persuasion that the governor would look a fool if he didn't give Gloria a pardon.

"Aren't you at all excited about that?"

Sarah paused to determine if she would be excited over the plate of snow crab. Even before she got in trouble, she never really fancied herself worthy of such a dish. She thought that it was too high a reach for trailer-park trash to expect, let alone indulge in.

That's what she considered herself. She was one of the million plus who smoked cheap cigarettes, drank cheap box wine, robbed cable off the neighbors and lounged in the front lawn on broken lawn chairs. That was the stereotype that she identified with. Now she had been thrown into a pit of struggling students and hard-charging future execs.

She smiled at the thought that her name was drawn. The prize could have been a slinky and she would have been just as happy. It was the feeling of being included that brought her joy—being included in something that carried energy.

This was not the type of energy discussed in physics, extracted out of the air or from the ground. No mechanism could measure the joules of its potential or spent energy. It was harder to see than the wind. The wind at least had the elements of oxygen, nitrogen and carbon dioxide to indicate its intent. Wind wasn't detectable up close. The result of its presence could only be seen as it moved, picking things up, twirling them around and setting them back down.

This energy could be felt when the hair stood up on the back of the neck, or with an undetectable vibration in the air like at a church service, a sports event or a concert. This was the energy that excited Sarah's nerves. To be wanted meant more to her than anything she could think of. This wasn't the *wanted* like a previous boyfriend who showed her faux passion for three minutes, then rolled over. It was someone cheering for her who had nothing to gain in the event. It was the sincere joy they felt for her. Something as rare to her life as a blue moon in her twenty years of existence.

"Yeah. I think I'm excited. I really wasn't holding out much hope for anything," Sarah said.

"C'mon, Miss Sarah, let's get to class before we're late," Helen said. "I wonder who the mystery guest is."

"I don't know. Could be anyone, really, knowing the ties that Dean Vickery seems to have. You're looking good though. How much weight have you lost?"

"I don't know."

"You don't?"

"I asked the PA to keep that information from me until I'm ready to graduate." Helen gathered her books and prepared to leave their room.

"Then how do you keep track to see if you're on track to meet your goals?" Sarah joined her as they made their way through the hallways to the classrooms.

"Anna and I developed a chart that I use to rate myself on how I feel. Like how much energy I feel at the beginning, middle and end of the day. I also write down what I accomplished. I write down my mood, if I was depressed or happy, anxious or calm."

"So how do you know that you're making progress?" Sarah asked as they turned the corner into the main hall.

"Miss Anna is working on her doctorate degree. Me and a few others are her guinea pigs for her dissertation. The categories are weighted, and we are shown a printout with an overall score and a chart that tracks how far we've come since we stepped onto campus grounds."

"I haven't heard of it. Why didn't they group everyone into this program?" Sarah fell back behind Helen so they could skirt around a group of women waiting to be let into a classroom.

"I think it's a pilot program. They're just testing it on a small number of people," Helen said.

"Is the counseling any different?" Sarah asked.

"No. All that is the same, she told me. The scoring system is the only new thing."

"Who else is in the program?"

"We're not allowed to say, even if we know. They say it's a trust issue. We can divulge that we are in it but not anyone else. It's not our story to tell. That's what Miss Gearda told me. For all I know, I may be the only one here."

"Only one here?"

"I know she works elsewhere outside the academy. I'm just putting two and two together is all."

"I see. Why do you think they chose you?"

"I think maybe because I ratted on myself."

"Ratted on yourself?"

"Before all my trouble began, I started to see that my boyfriend was using me. I didn't have the courage to leave or kick him out. For months, I was depressed, I just didn't know it. When I couldn't take it anymore, I found his gun. Five nights in a row, I put that gun to my head. I couldn't even pull the trigger.

"The fifth night, he caught me. We argued, then he beat me. He forced more drugs into me, then beat me some more. I fell on the floor. I don't remember anything after that. They said that I dialed nine one one. In the background they heard a man cussing and an occasional thump when he would kick me."

"Oh my god," Sarah said, shocked at what had been caught on tape.

"They said that all I would say was 'Please shoot me,' over and over and over. It took them almost an hour to find me."

"That's insane." Sarah slowed her stride a beat to evaluate her roommate.

"After the hospital, I sat in county medical for a while. In my arraignment, I begged the judge to sentence me to die. She said my crime wasn't anywhere serious enough for capital punishment. She wouldn't allow it even if it was."

"What happened after that?"

"They sent in counselor after counselor to try and figure out what was wrong with me, and what to do with me. They tried pouring drugs down me to prop me up. I refused them. I refused to eat. I was disgusted with myself, with where I was, with everything. I wanted to quit hurting."

"I know how you feel." Sarah thought back to her own troubled life. "I don't know if I wanted to end everything like you did. I thought that if I fell asleep and didn't wake up, I wouldn't mind. Later, I just tried to push everyone away. I wanted to be left alone.

"I guess that's why I became violent. I just wanted to chase everyone away. Especially those who hurt me," Sarah confided.

"Your parents?" Helen asked.

"Yeah, and boyfriends," Sarah said.

"Why didn't you just leave?"

"I don't know. Maybe because I felt trapped. No money, no plan to go anywhere." Sarah turned the conversation in on herself, saying softly, "Not knowing how life could be so different or that I could be a part of that if I wanted."

"What will we know tomorrow, right?" Helen commented, coming to a stop outside their classroom.

"What happened after the counselors?"

"I tried to will myself to die. As I lay on the floor in medical."

"On the floor?"

"I thought I could get hypothermia from lying on the floor."

Sarah chuckled. "Really. Wow, you were desperate to die. I think that would have taken a long time."

"It's funny now," Helen said.

"I'm glad you're taking it well."

"I am. It's weird, though. It's like even though I was an adult, I was looking at my past as if I were a parent looking down on their child. I did a lot of stupid things and have to wonder what I was thinking to do something like that."

"True. I think everyone goes through something like that—some of us just a little later in life." Sarah grumbled the second part more to herself than to Helen.

"My pivotal moment came while I was lying on the floor," Helen continued. "I could hear that song off of *Sister Act 2*; I can't think of the title. It says something about if you want to make something of yourself, you have to stand up and pay attention."

"Miss Helen, it's called 'Pay Attention.' "

"It is? Anyway, that song soaked into me and became my driving force to become someone different. I asked my defense attorney if I could be sentenced to one of their boot camps. I knew that straight jail time would not allow me to change like I wanted to.

"She talked to the judge, asking for their state-run boot camp. To enter it, I would have had to lose almost a hundred pounds, then they would have fed me large amounts of food. I told her that I wanted to do my time, but I also wanted to change my life so I wouldn't fall back into that same old rut.

"The judge sent me back to the jail and ordered me back the following day. When I came back, she said that she had made a call to Dean Vickery and asked him to send someone up to interview me. Now here I am." Helen ended her story with a wisp of positive bubbly energy.

"Miss Helen, I'm proud of you. You've done the most amazing turnaround."

"Thank you. You have too, Miss Sarah."

****

"What's an Oxford comma?" Sarah asked, coming out of her trance. Studying the passage and trying to condense it to fewer than ninety words without losing all pertinent information was harder than Sarah had thought.

Helen peered up from her own studies. Since everything was self-paced, she had already done the exercise that Sarah was working on: reducing a lengthy, wordy document down to something that was clear and concise, but still maintaining the necessary description. "It's a comma that is optional. If you use it, you must use it throughout the document," Helen said.

"Oh. Kinda like the academy. Either you're all in or you're going to prison for a very long time."

"Exactly."

"What are you working on?"

"Translating William Cuthbert Faulkner."

"Is he German?"

"No. He's from Mississippi. The assignment is to take these ridiculously complex words and translate them into something that the everyday reader can understand without thumbing through the dictionary three times per sentence."

"So, I get to look forward to that?"

"Yes, ma'am."

"Wonderful," Sarah said sarcastically.

"Excuse me, ladies."

Sarah and Helen looked up to find Gearda standing next to their table.

"May I speak to you in private, Miss Sarah?"

"Oh god. Anytime someone says those words, it usually means bad news."

Miss Gearda didn't respond. She just stood patiently. Sarah closed her books with her papers stuck in the middle as a placeholder, got up and followed the head counselor out into the hall.

"There's no easy way to tell you this."

Sarah's mind immediately bolted to concern for Gloria. If something had happened to her, she would never forgive herself. All the months of being good and trying hard would be for nothing. She wanted to show Gloria that she was worth the effort and sacrifice. She knew she was supposed to do this for herself. Her old self would have flipped off every authority figure and parked her growing posterior in a comfortable spot, permanently freezing a "make me" expression on her face—but she wasn't that person anymore. She didn't know exactly who she was now. If left to her own devices, she would gravitate back to that old lifestyle and the familiarity it entailed. For now, she had just one overriding objective: get Gloria home to her family. Sarah mentally braced herself for the gut-wrenching horror that was about to be delivered.

She took a deep breath to calm herself like she had been taught, steadied her nerves and looked at Miss Gearda.

"Sarah, your mother passed away."

Sarah stood unblinking. Her breathing stopped. All neurons ceased to fire. "Gloria?" Sarah finally sputtered, color draining from her face.

"No. Your birth mother, Charlotte."

Sarah's brow scrunched together. She looked at Gearda, trying to digest what she'd just said.

"Are you okay?" Gearda asked.

Sarah nodded. "I think I just need some time to process this. May I have a pass to the atrium for a while?"

Chapter XIV

Unless incoming students knew how professional kitchens worked, they might be misled to believe that they are a madhouse of potential and kinetic energy as a multitude of people boiled through the kitchen, almost but not quite colliding with each other. Like water boiling in the soup pot churning the vegetables, meat and spices, each person did their part to stimulate the customers' noses.

The culinary school was inertia based.

The guiding unspoken principle was to work hard and make the head chef shine so she could leave sooner and allow the next in line to step up to the hot plate. The freshman class was composed of the six most recent phase one graduates. Elizabeth was now on the hot plate.

She had studied everything she could find on restaurant management, learning to balance customers, finance and management with integrity. She took leadership courses to learn how to inspire those under her to do their best to make the whole team look good. She pored through the class on interior design, learning how to create an inviting atmosphere. She aced her classes on food preparation, health and hygiene.

She also devoured all the cooking shows she could, sometimes getting into arguments with other students who wanted to watch something else during the limited Sunday afternoon recreation time. She followed all their lessons and practiced their techniques, then experimented with how she could make them her own.

She had passed on what she could about cooking to the underclassmen and had mastered technique after technique shown to her by the academy's in-house culinarian.

Elizabeth made a final walk-through, checking each table, place setting, drapery and piece of artwork on the walls. She checked each server's uniform, adjusting a collar on one. Each server's hair had a unique combination ladder-and-waterfall braid that was arranged by the student stylists earlier that day.

"Well, ladies," she said, stepping back and addressing the serving crew. "This is our big show. You'll have many more, but this is my final one. Here, anyway. Everyone knows their assignments?"

Heads nodded, followed by "Yes, Chef Elizabeth." It was a title given her at the conclusion of the previous dinner a month prior. For the month leading up to her final challenge, she planned every dish being served, every spice that was sprinkled on each dish, the arrangement of each table. She supervised the vegetable harvest in the garden that morning and the arrival of the snow crab that she bought with her own earned "prison" wages and a matching donation from the dean's own pocket.

Elizabeth insisted that Dean Vickery be given a plate of snow crab without having to go through the drawing. He insisted that he would take his chances like everyone else. He did not draw one of the prestigious plates.

Elizabeth dismissed the hostess and servers to take up their stations. The doors would open in five minutes, and she walked through the temporary swinging doors to check on her cooking staff.

A pan clattered to the floor on the far side of the kitchen. "What was that?" Elizabeth asked across the kitchen staff.

The junior and senior staff churned like a boiling pot. A knife thumped rhythmically on a cutting board. Steam billowed up into the exhaust fans. A couple of spoons clattered against stainless mixing bowls. Elizabeth stopped by each station, tasting, smelling and checking the textures of her masterfully designed menu. This was, in a sense, her final exam. She would be flying over that final fence very soon.

Her little brother, mother and favorite uncle had arrived that morning. She spent a few minutes with them before she had to return to the kitchen. She relished the letters from her uncle, as they were the most encouraging for the direction she wanted to go. *Your business plan, menu ideas and passion for cooking are key ingredients for a successful restaurant. If your fellow students and I like your cooking, you've got yourself a business partner.*

Her uncle, Danny Jacobs, had been a notable food critic a decade before; now he was semiretired and investing in commercial properties and start-ups. She wanted to impress him more than anyone else. Not because of the money he held and the opportunity that he offered, but for the rare chance to see him smile. That was one of the top reasons she poured all her effort into this event—to see a radiant smile spread across his lips. He was very particular about his food and rarely smiled about anything and even less frequently over food.

Danny refused the snow crab. "If your other menu items are good, I have no doubt that the crab will be delightful." He gave Elizabeth the slightest of a wink—a motion that told her "I believe in you," and "bring it." He was a tough, shrewd man, a Marine Corps veteran, a purple heart recipient and a professional bachelor. She didn't know why she was drawn to him. He was a boring statue, and she was a bubbly ball of energy, but for some reason they worked well together.

Elizabeth stepped out of the kitchen and looked at the clock on the wall. Twenty seconds ticked by as she watched the second hand climb its way to the top of the six o'clock hour.

"Open the doors," Elizabeth said.

****

Sarah watched as pink, blue and yellow butterflies fluttered from flower to flower. She had come to the atrium expecting to bawl her eyes out; instead, she laughed. It wasn't a laugh like she was glad the woman was gone. It wasn't mean-spirited at all. If anything, it was a "damn the luck" type of laugh. She didn't know if she felt pity for herself or for her mother. Sarah still wished Charlotte wasn't her mother.

She also wished Charlotte's eyes could have been opened to a broader world of understanding instead of lurking in the depths of a bottle. Maybe it was her own way of punishing herself. Maybe she couldn't find the courage to walk out with nothing. Maybe she just wasn't a strong-willed person to begin with.

After Sarah's laughter died off, she watched the butterflies, and her thoughts drifted to Gloria. She wondered if Gloria had sat in the atrium to watch them as well. She replayed all the events from phase one in her mind, searching for anything that she might have missed—any message that she could cling to, to let her know she was on the right path. She remembered how Gloria had held her and let all the pent-up fear, anger and sadness escape through her tears, and how she had comforted Sarah even though her arm had been broken, yet not a tear was shed for her injury.

At times, she tried to force her thoughts back to her mother, deciding that that was the reason she was allowed to sit among the plants and trickling waterfall. Students could sit only on the benches. They weren't allowed to touch the plants or insects. If a butterfly were to land on a student, she wasn't to move until it flew off or a gentle breath of air coaxed it to find another resting spot.

"How are you doing, Miss Sarah?"

Sarah jumped at the sudden noise. Her wandering mind was ripped back to the present. "I don't know."

Gearda walked closer and sat down on the opposite end of the bench. "Do you need some help understanding something? You seem a bit puzzled, and your eyes aren't puffy like you've been crying."

"Honestly, I haven't been crying. I don't know why. I thought I wanted to come in here, cry my eyes out and grieve like any normal person would do. Then get back to life."

"So, what did you do instead?"

"I laughed." Sarah ducked her head, ashamed for doing something that wasn't typical or expected, thinking that it was the wrong answer and that she would be punished for it.

"There are many different reasons to laugh, and the causes are just as many. Of course, the most common one is when something is funny. Others are like aha moments. I've even read a story from the Vietnam War where a platoon was cornered at the top of a hill. Severely outnumbered. They held their ground by throwing rocks and shooting the enemy as they jumped, thinking they were grenades. They even tried a big, belly horselaugh, and it gained them several moments of silence while the enemy tried to understand why.

"So, you seem ashamed that you did laugh. Can you tell me how you felt while you were laughing?"

Sarah thought for a long moment. "It wasn't a joyful laugh. It wasn't one of 'karma caught you.' It was a laugh similar to that of the first day of spring when you open the windows and let the musty stench of winter escape and let the fresh fragrance of new life in."

"Wow. That's really perceptive. What happened next?"

"I thought of Gloria, hoping that I'm doing right by her."

"Do you think that you are?"

"I think so. I don't know. I'm doing everything that I'm told, following all the rules. I can see what I want, but I don't see the step-by-step directions."

"Go on," Gearda said when the lengthening pause implied a response.

"That's just it. I don't know if I'm doing this right. I don't want to get all the way to the end only to find a dead end. All that time wasted when she could be home where she belongs."

"When who should be home?"

"Gloria," Sarah said with a tense voice.

A butterfly landed on Sarah's hand. Both Gearda and Sarah froze, watching the innocent creature display its brilliant colors. A black dot on its forewing broke up the solid blue field of its fore and hind wings. On the outer margin of the wing, a golden yellow line arced upward, paralleling its black antennae and bordering the field of blue.

"Seems like someone has some empathy for you."

Sarah lifted her hand slowly. "Thank you, my little friend." It paused only a moment longer before fluttering away to join the kaleidoscope of colors churning around the yellow, white and red flowers.

"So, you still feel guilty about Gloria being sent away."

"Yes." Sarah started to pull her feet up on the bench to hide her embarrassment, but then remembered the No Feet on the Bench rule posted on either side of the atrium. "Does it ever go away?"

"I can't tell you that. Everyone is different. If anything at all could happen to help your guilt go away, what would it be?"

Sarah huffed. "For me to go to prison instead of her."

"That is survivor's guilt. What else is there?"

"I can get her a pardon."

"Yes."

"That's what I've been working on. I've sent letters to everyone I can think of to write to the governor. I've only gotten one letter back saying that he is a very busy man and that the application is waiting for his review."

"How does that make you feel?"

"Like no one takes me seriously. Like I'm a good-for-nothing inmate. Like the truth doesn't matter and it's all in how you play the game. It's like in order to win, you have to be more corrupt than the next guy, yet still fly under the radar. I understand that people will tell you anything to save their own skin. I used to be one of them.

"I would play one boyfriend against the other just to get sympathy or something that I wanted downtown. Or, I would pin the blame on them and play the helpless victim. I went as far as playing sick so they would clean the house and cook dinner after they worked all day.

"But, that's not me anymore. I've changed. I know I have, because I wouldn't seek this much solitude."

"Why do you suppose you seek solitude?"

Sarah sighed, growing weary of the conversation. She knew the answer. She had said it several times before in previous counseling sessions. "Because it's a small way I can punish myself and not be around anyone else to harm them and have to feel guilty for that also."

Birds chirped in the distance. A honeybee joined the butterflies seeking the sweet nectar within the blooms.

"If you stay away from people, yes, there is less risk of being hurt or hurting someone, but you lose out on the joy too."

"What do you mean?"

"How did you feel when Miss Harley sailed through the obstacle course wearing your shoe?"

Sarah smiled while remembering the tiny girl flying through the air as graceful as the hummingbird that just appeared in the atrium. She smiled at both the bird and the memory. "Would I have gotten in trouble for the shoe if she failed to take that rope back up?"

"It's hard to say. I guess the chances for that would be greater if she did fail. Though I couldn't say for sure. So, what did you feel?"

"Dread, at first."

"Why?"

"Because I wanted to do the right thing."

"And was that the right thing to do?"

"Yes. Yes, it was," Sarah said with conviction.

"So, after the dread, what did you feel?"

"Exhilaration."

"So, because you elected to be around people, you got to share in a wonderful experience. You never know when something great will come about. In a way, life is like gambling—you can't win unless you play. But, throwing money at the casino table hoping to win is not good. We want you to understand the degree of risk before you make your decision.

"That's our job here. We want you to evaluate life's decisions and make educated choices. Do you understand what I'm trying to say?"

"Yes, Miss Gearda."

"Now, I'm going to take an educated guess and say that there is some really delicious snow crab down the hall. Would you care to join me? I drew one of the tickets too."

Sarah looked up unenthusiastically at the head counselor. "Thank you, Miss Gearda, but honestly, I would trade that snow crab for a five-minute audience with the governor."

"Are you sure?"

"Yes, ma'am. I want to get my mind right so I can get back to my studies and not be distracted. May I have a bit more time in here?"

"I'll have someone come get you when we're done. You'll be locked in this section of the building until then."

"Yes, ma'am."

"I'll notify control to keep an eye on you."

"Yes, ma'am. Thank you."

****

"You're a little bit late." Dean Vickery stood and pulled Gearda's seat out for her. The aroma of all the food coupled with the makeshift elegance of the decor transformed the basic cafeteria into a quaint dining establishment.

"I was checking in on Sarah Menendez," Gearda said, unfolding her napkin and placing it on her lap.

"How's she doing?"

"She's alright." Gearda then flagged down a server. "Tell Chef Elizabeth that Miss Menendez won't be joining us."

Dean Vickery waited for the server to go, then turned to Gearda. "She's not coming to this?"

"No. She's still working through some things."

"Wasn't her name drawn for a crab dinner?"

"Yes. She said she would trade it for a five-minute audience with the governor. I think she's having trouble getting people to listen to her and take her seriously."

"Unfortunately, some people label others 'once a screwup, always a screwup.' You're certain she won't be joining us?"

"I'm sure. I checked in on her from the control room just before coming here. She's in no condition to come here and be festive."

"You are checking on her after this, correct?"

"Yes. Of course."

"Good. You can tell her that I'll take the trade," Dean Vickery said with a glint in his eyes.

"How's Elizabeth doing?" Gearda asked. Taking a wedge of flat bread covered with avocado and parsley salsa and setting it on her plate, she glanced across the room to see smiling faces and excited chatter.

"She has a challenge on her hands." Danny Jacobs's deep baritone voice caught Gearda off guard, as he had only a slight build. He was a handsome gentleman with plenty of gray in his short-cropped hair. "One of her sous-chefs got a concussion and two others got some nasty burns."

"Oh my gosh. Are they going to be okay?" Gearda asked.

"They said that they should be fine. One should be back already," a young, fair-skinned man said, repeating part of the table's earlier conversation.

"Miss Gearda, this is Gilson and Patty Henderson," Dean Vickery said, gesturing to the other people at the table. "Elizabeth's mother and younger brother."

"It's a pleasure to meet you." Gearda smiled at the two. "Are you excited to see your sister again?"

Gilson looked up to the woman. He giggled a bit. "Yes." Gearda recognized the unmistakable features of Down syndrome, but he seemed to speak more precisely and thoughtfully than what she had originally perceived. His cognitive functions seemed sharper than those of the clients with Down syndrome she had worked with before.

Dean Vickery flagged down a server and instructed her to bring him Sarah's snow crab ticket. Once in his hand he inspected it for a brief moment, then stood. He tapped the butter knife on his glass to quiet the crowd and attract their attention. Elizabeth heard the ting of the glass and stepped out of the kitchen, as she knew that the dean would want to make a short speech before the main course was brought out.

"Ladies. It is with great pleasure that we are able to come together like this and enjoy a wonderful event with delicious food. Chef Elizabeth has worked tirelessly to tantalize our palates with exquisite tastes and textures. Our mystery guest is running a little late, but I'm told that they are close and will be here shortly.

"Those who are wondering who the next chef will be will have to wait until dinner is finished. As always, we have the comment cards in the center of the table. Please comment on each part of your dining experience. Doesn't matter if it was good or bad, it just matters that you're honest.

"Please say what you liked or didn't like. Give a suggestion if you have one. That is how good businesses operate. They need your feedback so they can constantly improve and maintain excellent service. We set the bar high here so you can be your best out there."

A round of applause approved the message. A server came up and whispered in Dean Vickery's ear.

"Ladies and gentlemen," he said, directing the second part to the only other males in the room, more specifically the two sitting at his table. "As most of you have heard, we have a mystery guest who, I am told, is as excited to meet you as you are wondering who he is. He is exceptionally talented both on-screen and in a courtroom. Most of you don't know his skill in the courtroom, but I'm sure you remember him from your youth as Micky Michael, Kid Detective.

"Please welcome the Honorable David Schrader."

The doors opened to a smaller-than-average size man. He wore a casual blue suit and polished black loafers. His full head of hair still carried the short mussed-up look that made him popular in the hit TV sitcom from his youth. Wisps of gray accented his temples. Wrinkles started their stronghold at the corners of his eyes. He entered the dining hall to a grand applause from everyone in the room. Shaking the occasional hand, he made his way to Dean Vickery's table.

Chapter XV

Jamika sat back, frustrated that the flimsy plastic tube pen quit writing again. Getting up off the padded floor, she knocked on the bathroom cupboard door. Though she wasn't allowed to talk to anyone, the simple coded tapping supplied the necessary things she needed to write her letters of apology. The hardest letter for her to write was the one she addressed to her deceased daughter. Each page became wrinkled from dozens to hundreds of tears, making the stack of forty-seven pages even harder to cram into an already oversize envelope.

The single bulb burned brightly in the center of the ceiling, never blinking. It stared down on her as she wrote carefully while trying to articulate thoughts, and wildly when her emotions gripped her soul. She hadn't felt anxiety over any of her other letters, as they were written to those she had affected, apologizing for her behavior and asking for forgiveness.

This letter made her soul run in a blind panic. Her palms were sweaty, and her breath was ragged and uneven as she scribbled lines communicating her thoughts. She didn't want to write it, but she knew she would die if she didn't. To leave this question unasked, and worse, unanswered, hinged her on bliss or mental self-destruction.

"Goddamn pen," she muttered to herself. She knew she was almost done. She just needed to ask one final question. If she didn't ask it, she would surely die. If she did ask it, she had a fifty-fifty shot. A *yes* meant she had something to live for; a *no* meant the death of her soul.

It was Saturday night. Jamika didn't know of the celebrity in the house, or that all the students and most of the staff were dining on snow crab. It wouldn't have mattered anyway, because her future was on the line and, to her, the stakes had never been higher. She knew she couldn't put in sappy stuff like "I'll die without you." She had to be sincere without being sappy.

Dozens of pages were crumpled up and tossed in the garbage, a.k.a. the floor. After having mulled over her mission days before, she addressed the first letter to the dean.

Sir, I've been an ass. Please forward all the following pages to Miss Gearda. Thank you for the kick in the ass. Jamika.

The pages that followed were those to her daughter, a few to her fellow students and teachers and the final one was to, she hoped, her future.

****

Dean Vickery flipped through the final tear-stained pages. "What do you think?" He leaned back in his chair, scratching his temple with the end of his pen.

Gearda set the page she was studying back on his desk. "I think her emotions are stable enough for now. She needs a significant reason to solidify them in place though."

118

"That's what I'm seeing also. It all comes down to that one question."

"What if she doesn't get the answer she wants?"

"Then we pick up the pieces and start gluing them back together."

"Can we sidestep this in any way?"

"No. I don't think so. I think this is going to be full throttle toward a cliff. We're either going to have one hell of a mess at the bottom or we'll get to watch an eagle fly."

"I guess there's not much more we can do except watch and pray."

"I believe you're right." Dean Vickery leaned forward with his pen and scribbled his signature on the order.

****

Jamika twisted her fingers over and over while biting her bottom lip until it started to bleed. She stood in the hall just around the corner from supply, listening for anyone coming in to pick up or leave mail or packages. She peeked around the corner at the slightest sound looking for the solid brown uniform.

****

A buzz at the door prompted Jamika to look around the corner of the hall. She watched Rebecca unlock it. But instead of the brown uniform she sought, a blue and white uniform stepped through the opening. Jamika's heart hit the floor. Loud laughter ignited in the small room and she knew the one she sought wasn't present. If he didn't come today, she was afraid she would lose her mind to the perpetual crazy house looming just out of sight in her mind. Closing time was approaching fast along with a certified meltdown.

Jamika slid down the wall, preparing for the onslaught of emotions to rip her apart. She could hear Rebecca talking to the delivery driver.

"Oh. Let me get that for you," Jamika heard her say. The click from the door latch and the small squeak from the hinge told her that the driver was leaving.

"Hello. You're running late."

Jamika's heart stopped. She listened intently for any sound, then heard the rattle of a hand truck as it bounced and thudded into the receiving office.

"Yes. Right there is fine," Rebecca said. "Is there any more? I've been waiting for a large shipment from Eloquine Educational Supplies. They're the new lab experiments for the chemistry and physics classes."

Jamika strained in earnest to hear any answer, whether verbal or the scratching of a pen. She couldn't read sign language, but if her dreams were realized, she would be more than happy to learn.

"No. These are the only ones that need to go."

It had to be now. He was leaving. She might not get another chance. If he left without seeing her, she didn't know what she would do. Her life would be worthless and boring and sad and gut-wrenching. She heard the squeak of the door again. He was leaving—she had to move now. Her legs froze in place and she cowered just out of sight. Tears boiled forth at her sudden paralysis.

****

Landon was in a hurry. There were dozens more packages today and he had gotten a flat tire that put him seriously behind schedule. He had expressed as much to Rebecca, so she busied herself with putting away the packages that he brought.

A simple white envelope sat on top of the stack of boxes going out. He started to turn and ask why it didn't have a shipping label, then noticed one word printed on the front. It was his name.

Turning over the envelope, he lifted the unsealed flap and pulled out the paper. Taped to the center was the *Peanuts* comic strip he had tried to give to Jamika hoping to possibly start writing letters back and forth and, one day, win a first date. He hadn't expected her to rip it and wad it up.

Dean Vickery promised him that he would have her apologize for her actions and return the comic in as good a shape as possible. Now it was laminated and taped in the middle of the sheet.

He had wondered why he kept thinking of her. He asked his grandmother as much. "You probably need something that she has," she told him. He tried to get her to elaborate, but she wouldn't budge any more on the subject.

Above the comic was a message. *I've been a huge jerk to you. I am sorry.* Landon smiled at the sincere apology until he read the bottom of the page.

****

Jamika slowly walked around the corner. The shaved head of the man glistened in the florescent light as he stood immobile like a statue. The packages sat on the hand truck on the floor. The outside door had closed, preventing the alarm from alerting the whole campus of a possible escape. She didn't see the point, as the control room monitored the secondary gate just outside and had to approve every entry and exit.

Landon stood stock still. Jamika waited with every nerve screaming to explode. His head rose and he turned. She had seen him numerous times before but hadn't had any inclination to get to know him. She was only temporary and would be hundreds of miles away when finished with the program.

Now she had no place to go. She felt herself in the blackest of caves with only a single light far in the distance. She hoped and prayed that it was her way out, her salvation and the key to her aching heart.

She kept her gaze on his chin. It was strong and confident just like the rest of him. He had a type of gentle strength that she had not encountered before. It drew her in, caressing her soul to feel at ease and excited at the same time. She wanted to know more about him, yet she knew that this was the man she needed in her life; therefore needing to know more was unnecessary. For the moment, her attention was riveted to the cleft of his chin under his brilliant white teeth. She had missed the moment when he smiled. She wanted to see that first hint of a smile and she had missed it. That moment was gone now and would never come around again.

Her eyes jumped to his. They too were smiling just as radiant as his teeth. Slowly he brought his right hand up from the note, curled it into a fist and nodded it up and down.

Jamika sought something more. Her instincts misfired and she didn't recognize the communication for what it was. Her nerves began to unravel. She didn't understand the smile, the bright eyes or the nodding fist.

"Jamika."

The sound only barely registered in her brain.

"Jamika!" Rebecca said, practically yelling.

She turned to look at Rebecca.

"That means yes."

Jamika looked back at the tall, well-groomed man. He was nodding his head.

"He said yes," Rebecca reiterated.

Jamika's nerves uncoiled into action. She knew she had to move. It was a requirement for the answer received. She had to do something. So, she did the first thing that came to mind. She bolted down the hall, away from Landon.

****

"Come in," Dean Vickery said to the knock on his door.

"Sir?"

"Yes. What can I help you with, Miss Harley?"

"Sir. The bathrooms in halls C, D and E are flooded."

"Why are they flooded?"

"I don't know, sir. I was sent to inform you that they were."

"Well, thank you. Come back and inform me when you find out why *and* have a solution underway."

"Yes, sir," Harley said, and ducked back out the door.

Dean Vickery rubbed his temples, forcing back the migraine that had suddenly pressed in on him. He opened his desk drawer and pulled out a bottle of headache medicine. Downing two of the pills, he tried to focus on the spreadsheet displayed on his computer screen. He rapped his knuckles on the hardwood, but the rapping continued when he stopped.

"Yes."

Gala, Dean Vickery's secretary, opened the door and poked her head in. "Sir, Mr. Allen and Miss Tina are here for your appointment."

"Thank you, Miss Gala. Please show them in." Dean Vickery straightened his desk and stashed a file away to be dealt with later. A fit woman wearing a black pantsuit accented with a purple scarf entered his office and made her way to one of the plush leather chairs next to the window. A squat, round man followed and sat in the second chair. He wore a gray suit that if fastened would burst open the moment he relaxed his exorbitant man-shed, launching the button across the room.

Settling into the meeting, they reviewed the past several months' analytics of the financial health of the academy. Going over all the accounts, Dean Vickery pointed at one. "What's happening with this account and its projections?"

"We lost that account," Tina said.

"What do you mean we lost one of our accounts?" Dean Vickery sat up in his chair.

"Freshstokk isn't renewing their contract," Allen Cole said. Allen was the newest member on the board of directors and an accountant by profession. He was still green in his position, having served only eight months on the board and having been in charge of financial reports.

"Why not?"

"They said that they found another organic produce supplier. They didn't give a specific reason," Allen said.

"Are they abiding by the contract?"

"Yes." Tina Hallsnic spoke up. She had been preparing to start the negotiations on their fourth two-year contract. "They gave us a written notice last week. I've tried talking with them every day since then, but I get vague answers or get shuffled back to the receptionist to set an appointment."

"Well, set an appointment. See if we can get this resolved."

"I already did. The appointment is two months out. If a deal is struck, that leaves little time to review the new contract, and payments could be delayed."

Dean Vickery sat in silence, contemplating the options. They had had a great relationship with Freshstokk and had done business together with very few problems. He creased his brow, trying to decipher why they weren't open to communication. The managers and owners had always been forthcoming about any changes and the reasons for them.

"I just don't see them—"

The door flew open and slammed against its doorstop, sending a rippling vibration through the oak and rattling a hinge loose. Jamika followed through and almost collided with the attorney. A blaze of exhilaration radiated from her core, influencing anything within her immediate area. Her eyes locked on Dean Vickery's, demanding an immediate response.

"Sir. Will you give me away?" Jamika yelled, interrupting the somber discussion.

"Bloody hell, woman. I'll give you to the bloody Kaiser if you would just leave this room." The intrusion had tipped Harold Vickery over the edge. It was rare that he lost his temper enough to dredge up the London accent and lingo from his mother's London roots.

His reddening face didn't dissuade Jamika from the glorious news she had just received. She vanished from the room as fast as she had appeared, then sprinted back down the hall toward shipping and receiving, leaving his door wide open.

The secretary, along with a small crowd, leaned to peek into the office, seeking an answer for the odd behavior.

"What the hell was that?" Allen Cole asked, peering up at Dean Vickery.

Dean Vickery hadn't moved, still trying to digest what the question had been. Recognizing the confusion on his face, Tina spoke up and filled in what was obvious to her but apparently not to Allen or to Dean Vickery. "Apparently there's going to be a wedding, and you're one of the star guests, dad."

Chapter XVI

Dawn entered Sarah's mind, though it was midafternoon. The numb state she had been in since learning that her mother had passed finally diminished enough for her to see the world around her. She had been carrying on as an automated object, going through the motions, giving only the basic of answers to what she was asked.

"Miss Sarah. What did you get for number eight?"

Sarah looked at the homework that she had completed last Friday. "I got x squared minus a over x."

"That is incorrect," said Mrs. Jenkins, the school's math professor. A strict but fair woman, she didn't tolerate any slacking off. Even with the self-paced guidelines, she found a way to make everyone adhere to her pristine code of conduct and keep her class together as one. "Come see me in your free time or track down one of the tutors. Moving on."

She didn't wait for anyone, describing time as the most precious commodity. In business, time was everything. She understood that no matter how rich people were, they couldn't buy back yesterday. So, it was in the students' best interests to listen the best they could on her time, then practice on their own time. She told them to work the problem a dozen times before asking for help, then a dozen more to solidify it the right way. They were also to write a sentence describing what they did wrong to help remind them about it in the future.

Sarah was close to taking the semester test and would be able to move on to business calculus. The bell rang, and she gathered her things to take back to her shared room and get ready for lunch. She found Temperance in the hall and waved a hand at her.

"Miss Temperance, how're the new CDL classes going?"

"They're going good now. At first, I didn't know what I was doing. We were supposed to take the tests on the computer, but the program crashed, and we had to wait for a tech to come out and fix it. The books helped while we were waiting, and I had my students just do the quizzes at the end of each chapter."

"That's great. Something seems different. Did I miss something?"

"Different? Since when?" Temperance was confused by her question.

"I don't know. I don't remember much since last Saturday when I found out my mom passed away."

"Oh. I'm so sorry. I didn't know."

"I'm not sorry. She was a mean, unaffectionate woman. I don't know. Sometimes I wished her dead, but all I really wanted was for her to be the mom that so many other kids had but I didn't. I was always jealous of the parents that other kids had."

"I guess I can relate a little. After a while, I just wanted my mom to be normal and not push me into so many pageants. Seems she was the opposite of yours. She cared too much and tried to mold me into her image."

The two women smiled at their opposite backgrounds. "How was the dinner Saturday?" Sarah asked.

"Oh, it was delicious. I had the veal but was offered a small bite of the crab and it was heavenly. Dean Vickery auctioned off your crab dinner for charity."

"He did?"

"You know him. He won't let anything go to waste, especially that crab."

"So, who got it? How much did they pay?"

"He had everyone stand up who wanted it except those who already had a ticket. We had to sit down when the amount surpassed what we knew we could afford. I had to sit down after twenty dollars."

"How much did it go for?" Sarah asked.

"Two hundred and five."

"Wow. Someone must have wanted it bad."

"I know. Especially since we only get a dollar an hour and have to buy all of our personal items at regular store price."

"Aren't we supposed to get minimum wage?"

"We do. All but a dollar of that goes to the nest egg that we get when we complete the program."

"Oh yeah. I forgot about that. Anything else happen?"

"Dean Vickery announced two chefs for a head-to-head battle during next month's dinner."

"Head-to-head battle? What?"

They turned the corner into their dorm wing. "Yeah. They're supposed to design a series of meals where they will each cook their own version of a classic dish and present it to the student body for voting."

"I see. What about Elizabeth's uncle? What did he think of the food?"

"I heard that he was going to buy her a restaurant if he liked the food."

128

"Did he like it?"

"From the first bite he was grinnin' like a baby who just discovered he had toes," Temperance explained.

Sarah smiled. She was happy that someone was leaving here for bigger and better things, and for Elizabeth, tastier things. A pang of disappointment set in about having missed out on such a wonderful event. Though she chided herself for thinking that, she knew she wouldn't have made good dining company anyway.

If she had gone, she surmised that under the circumstances she wouldn't have enjoyed it as much as it deserved. She promised herself that she would seek out Elizabeth's new restaurant and order two of the most delicious things on the menu.

"Oh. I almost forgot. Who was the mystery guest?"

"Do you remember a show called Micky Michael, Kid Detective?"

Sarah furrowed her brow. "No, I don't. When did it air?"

"I think when I was in preschool, but there were reruns for a few years after."

"Oh. I wasn't allowed to watch TV when I was that young."

"Wow. Really?"

"Yeah. At the time, my mom was into some type of religious sect that thought the government was manipulating people through the TV, and her leader banned his congregation from watching," Sarah said.

"Seriously?"

"Yeah."

"I thought that stuff was only in the movies or some late-night documentary."

"It only lasted a few years. He moved away and we were left in poverty. Dad"—Sarah almost vomited at saying his name—"went into the police academy and got a job with the city. I was still young and didn't understand why, but after two years where everyone was happy, my parents suddenly started having nightly arguments. Then one day they stopped.

"I remember my mother started drinking heavily. She didn't argue anymore; she was just cold and distant from then on."

"Oh. I see," said Temperance.

"Back to Micky Michael. What's his real name?" Sarah asked.

"David Schrader."

"Oh. What did he do?"

"He told his story about the fast rise to fame, the fall when he got hooked on drugs. The time he served, his readdiction, his—"

"Wait. Wait. 'Readdiction?' Is that even a word?" Sarah asked.

"I don't know. That's the word that Judge Schrader used."

"Okay. Go on." Sarah dodged a student coming the opposite direction down the hall.

"The first time, the courts made him go through a treatment program. It didn't stick. He said he got tired of looking over his shoulder, wondering if someone was going to notice that he had returned to his old crutch. He said the anxiety was eating him up, and his agent couldn't find him any new acting jobs. He didn't want to chance turning himself in and facing more charges. He didn't want to go straight to rehab; he said he wanted to find something that would give him a bigger incentive."

"I'm guessing he found one."

"He went to talk with the judge that sentenced him. Waited in the back of the courtroom until he was done for the day. The judge invited him back to his office and they talked into the evening.

"He said that that was the moment he became fascinated with the law. The judge said that if he completed the treatment program, he would buy his college books for the first year. After he completed the first year, the same judge paid his tuition for the second year.

"He went on to law school, graduated, worked at a couple law firms, the DA's office and was recently appointed to be one of the civil judges in Saint Louis," Temperance concluded.

"Dang. He sure fast-tracked it," Sarah commented.

"That was the whole premise of his speech."

"What was?"

"He said 'ambition with a plan' will take us further than we would have thought possible. He said that we are no longer inmates, but just like with any good business deal, we have to fulfill our government-appointed contracts. He said that that's the root of good business."

"That makes sense," Sarah agreed.

"Hello, ladies." Gearda strolled up to Sarah and Temperance just outside the cafeteria. "Smells good. What are they serving?"

"I think it's Salisbury steak today," Temperance said.

"Sounds wonderful. Sarah, I have some good news for you."

"Yes, Miss Gearda?" Sarah inquired. She couldn't think what kind of good news she could get. She wasn't expecting anything she could immediately think of.

"Come see me in my office when you're finished with lunch," Gearda said, as she scribbled out a note giving Sarah permission to miss her next class.

"Yes, ma'am."

"Enjoy. See you in a bit, Miss Sarah."

"Yes, ma'am."

Sarah eyed two shaved heads standing in front of her in line. Their once scowling faces had transformed into happy chatter. Sarah didn't recognize them until she thought about the fight they seemed to have gotten mixed up in during her first few days of phase two.

"Miss Shandel, Miss Catrina, I thought you guys were like mortal enemies."

"Oh, hey Miss Sarah. We're friends," Shandel said, turning to Sarah.

"But you argue all the time."

"Oh, that was our bantering," Catrina said. "We were egging each other on. As in helping support each other."

Confusion spread across Sarah's face. "I don't understand."

Shandel twisted her mouth, thinking how to explain it. "Think of it this way. If someone says you can't do something and you want to prove them wrong, you put all your effort into proving them wrong and you find that you accomplished more than if you were left to do it on your own."

"Having resistance and a stubborn attitude can actually be the best thing," Catrina added.

Sarah puzzled at her words.

"You should know this firsthand," Shandel said.

"Know what?"

"Miss Sarah, you're famous for diving straight into adversity just to prove someone wrong," Catrina said.

"What?" Sarah stood perplexed, searching for the answer that seemed obvious to Shandel and Catrina.

"When you packed all those boulders to the top of the hill to complete Miss Gloria's assignments," Shandel said, turning back to the cafeteria line.

"Everyone respects you for that. The drills told you to do one thing and you pushed back and did what was right. If you think about it, would you have been able to accomplish what you did if they weren't in your face telling you to give up?" Catrina concluded.

"Resistance makes you stronger," Temperance added. "My father has told me that on a number of occasions. It's true."

Sarah shuffled down the line, thinking about the words and wisdom she had just heard.

****

"Come on in, Miss Sarah." Dean Vickery stood up from one of the three hard plastic chairs in Gearda's office. Gearda sat in her plush office chair. A third man sat to the far side of Dean Vickery. He wore a blue suit with a two-tone blue pinstripe tie. The woman who occupied the middle chair didn't say anything, but had an odd-shaped case sitting beside her chair.

"Sarah, this is Mr. Henderson and Miss Gilford."

Sarah shook each person's hand and greeted them, saying each person's name in turn to help her remember.

"Please sit," Dean Vickery invited.

"Yes, sir." Sarah sat in the chair and placed her hands palms down on her legs. The motion had become ingrained and automatic during the months she struggled in phase one. She wouldn't have noticed this time, except the man in the blue suit twisted a quizzical look across his face because of the oddity.

Dean Vickery noticed too. There was very little that he didn't notice. "Students are taught much of the same etiquette that the US Army teaches its new recruits. Like when seated, both hands are face down on their lap. Or when they are standing, they are either at attention with their hands flat at their sides and feet together, or feet apart and hands locked behind their back."

"What is the purpose of that?" the blue suit asked.

"It is a mixture of many different things. First, it's part of their contracts, but it is mostly a show of respect. Both to each other and to the rules of the house. They have to understand that with so many here, a higher sense of discipline is necessary for everyone to make the huge strides that we make."

The blue suit nodded and sat back, satisfied with the explanation. Dean Vickery's words set Sarah's mind a little more at ease. Her original thoughts of silly political games were gradually changing into a deeper understanding of the reasons why things were the way that they were. When people lived by themselves and were not dependent on the outside world, they could live as they saw fit. When more and more people came to live in close proximity, more rules, whether social or legal, became necessary to allow the most people possible to live in harmony.

"Miss Gearda."

"Yes, Miss Sarah."

"Miss Gearda. You said that there was some good news for me."

"Yes. Do you remember the conversation we had a few days ago in the atrium?"

"No, ma'am. Not particularly. I remember that we talked, but not much of what we said. I believe I've been in a daze for the last couple days, because I don't remember much of anything. I remember talking to Miss Temperance about her CDL class and a little about the dinner last Saturday."

"What did she say about the dinner?"

"She said that Miss Elizabeth's uncle was very happy about the food and that it was a very successful dinner." Sarah paused, waiting for someone else to interject and take the spotlight off of her. The short awkward silence urged her to continue. "She said the mystery guest was a movie star turned judge and that we are no longer inmates, but we still have to fulfill our contracts." Sarah turned to look at Dean Vickery. "Sir?"

"Yes, Miss Sarah."

"I don't understand. How are we not inmates?"

"I believe what Judge Schrader meant by that was that if you were to be released back into society now, there is a small chance that you would become part of the justice system again. That's why we screen people coming into the academy. First to evaluate their personality, then we put them through the boot camp phase to see if they have the determination to stay the course.

"Do you remember when you came to me and asked to finish for Miss Gloria?"

"Yes, sir."

"That is the moment when I knew you finally understood. With a little more grooming, I am confident that you will not have any more confrontations with the law. You would instead call them for assistance."

Sarah was shocked by Dean Vickery's vote of confidence when she wasn't even sure of herself.

"Even though you were ready to advance to stage two, the debt had to be satisfied. You took on that challenge and proved even more to me and others that you are a good candidate for this program. Does that make sense?"

"Yes sir, and thank you sir, for the opportunity to turn my life around."

"Remember, I revoked your application. It was the board and Miss Gloria who gave you the opportunity, but I am especially pleased that it's working out."

"Thank you sir, but I'm not sure it was for the best."

"Why do you say that?" Gearda asked.

"From what I hear, Gloria was an exceptional student and one deserving to be home with her family now. She doesn't deserve to be where she is."

"Sarah." Dean Vickery walked to the side of Gearda's desk so Sarah wouldn't have to turn in her seat. "Miss Gloria knew very well the consequences of her actions. She knew that she would be sent away, but she also knew that something had to be addressed at that time or it would hold you back for the rest of your life."

Sarah sat stone-faced, not knowing what to think or do.

"We had a long and detailed talk about what happened and why. She didn't want to see you or the academy fail. Those were her two priorities when we talked. She knew you were holding something back. She said that you were always tense like you were guarding against something."

"Yes sir, I was."

"She was prepared for the consequences. She knew what she was doing, so try not to fret over it too much."

"Yes sir, I'll try."

"Now, Miss Sarah. I told you that I have good news for you," Gearda said.

"Yes, ma'am." Sarah looked up apprehensively.

"You don't remember asking to trade your crab dinner for a five-minute audience with Governor Reynolds?"

Sarah sat for a minute, vaguely remembering the conversation. Her eyes suddenly shot to Gearda. Gearda's eyes directed Sarah's gaze to Dean Vickery.

Sarah looked up to the dean. "Sir?"

"When Miss Gearda told me about what you asked, I accepted the offer and auctioned off your plate."

"Sir?"

"I talked to Governor Reynolds on the phone this morning and he said he would arrange some time to meet. So, you'll have five minutes to make your argument."

Sarah exploded out of the chair and wrapped her arms around Dean Vickery's neck. She couldn't speak. She could only cry and crush the life out of the dean. The nightly anguish she felt for Gloria would soon be over. She hoped to sway the governor's mind and show him that if anyone deserved a pardon, it was Gloria Witcom.

Chapter XVII

Dean Vickery's shirt was now stained with Sarah's tears and a bit of rogue drool that had escaped with her sobbing. Sitting back in her chair, she apologized profusely about her unexpected behavior. After multiple statements were made to reassure her that it was quite understandable, she resumed her previous composure and sat at attention—this time with a smile on her face.

"I'm sorry to hear of your mother's passing. How are you doing with that news?" Dean Vickery asked.

Sarah hadn't expected the question, because she was largely indifferent and a bit happy at times—that woman was no longer around to cause her any more distress. Lately, most of her attention was focused on Gloria and how to get her safely home to her family.

"Sir, should I feel guilty if I smile because she's gone?"

"Why do you ask that? Can you elaborate on what you mean?" Gearda asked.

Sarah thought a bit. "Well it's like I'm happy that I know I will never have to feel threatened by her again. I'm sad because I'll never know what it is like to have a normal childhood. She and my father stole my innocence, and that's something I'll never be able to get back.

"I was angry at myself for a long time for not being a better daughter and for not being a son."

"Why do you feel anger for not being a son?" Gearda asked.

"How many times have you heard of the son being raped, versus the daughter?" Sarah said, fidgeting uncomfortably in her seat.

Mr. Henderson shrank backward at the uncomfortable topic in an ill attempt to distance himself from what he thought should be more of a private consultation. Dean Vickery blinked at Sarah's forwardness. She had transitioned from defiant to shy and was now showing a streak of confidence and courage. Miss Gilford quietly stood by the door, unfazed, because she was involved in corresponding with a colleague via her phone and didn't hear the escalating debate.

Gearda kept her professional composure with her notepad at the ready, as was her norm. "Miss Sarah, there's just no way of knowing those numbers. There are so many that go unreported."

"Miss Gearda, out of a hundred cases, how many have you *heard* of where the child in question was a male?"

"I really don't know."

"Please, Miss Gearda. Just a rough estimation."

"Maybe eight out of a hundred that I myself have heard of. The actual numbers may vary widely due to the nature that boys don't or won't tell of things like that to save the embarrassment of being stereotyped. So, to put it on a level playing field, I might say double or triple that percentage."

"So, for arguments sake let's say it is triple," Sarah said. "Instead of eight percent, it is now twenty-four percent. With those numbers, little girls are three times more likely to be molested than little boys are. That's just the ones you hear about and assume a higher number as you had stated. That's why at times I wish I came out a boy."

"I see," Gearda said.

"I'm assuming there's a reason that Mr. Henderson and Miss Gilford are here," Sarah said.

"Yes," Dean Vickery said, his face turning long. "Due to your mother's passing, the prosecutor doesn't have as solid of a case. She had worked out a deal to receive probation in return for her testimony. During the process of drying out for the conditions of the probation, her body somehow went into shock and she didn't recover from it. Each of her organs began to shut down, one right after the other.

"She was going to carry most of the weight in the prosecution's case, and it is set to go to trial, as your father wanted a trial by jury and denied any wrongdoing."

Sarah's blood began to boil at the thought of her father claiming innocence. "Don't you have the DNA evidence to support what happened?"

"That's another reason why we're here," Mr. Henderson said. "First, we're here to get a deposition from you and to tell you about the proceedings and what to expect. We're also here to take another DNA sample. Three, actually. The first one seems to have been tainted."

"You don't think that I gave birth." Sarah almost growled but checked herself and settled her nerves.

"Miss Menendez, we believe you. In fact, your DNA matches your daughter's DNA, but—" Mr. Henderson began, but stopped short at seeing Sarah's face drain of color and contort into anguish.

Sarah melted. Her chair could no longer contain her; she slipped off it and onto the floor. A nonbreathing crumpled pile of flesh fused with the floor. Grief tore at her face, threatening to shred flesh from bone. Gearda moved to comfort the barely gasping pile. Dean Vickery turned to Mr. Henderson and Miss Gilford, inviting them out into the hall to let Gearda handle the sobbing student.

Sarah's lungs pulled for air as her throat clenched to cut it off. She was oblivious to her surroundings as she began to wail, hammering her fist into the floor.

****

Sarah stared up at a familiar ceiling, first gaining an understanding of where she was, then piecing the events together of what she last remembered. "What happened?" Sarah whispered to herself as her eyes searched for more indications of what happened. She looked down to find her hands fastened to the hospital bed with heavy straps. The few minutes she had been awake listening brought nothing besides the distant hum of the ventilation system. Otherwise it was silent, with the lights dimly illuminating the small white-cloaked room, yet she felt a presence in the room.

"Did I hurt anyone?" Sarah finally called out to the room.

"No. Not that I heard," Ulyssa said, coming around to stand at the foot of Sarah's bed.

"What happened?"

"I don't know. You will have to ask Miss Gearda when she returns."

Sarah turned her head into the paper pillow, trying to hide her face from the embarrassment that had sent her into a flailing fit. She sobbed into the pillow. Ulyssa pulled a few tissues from a box, walked to the side of her bed and dried her tears.

"I heard that you lost your baby."

"Yeah, it was a long time ago," Sarah said, wishing the conversation would have ended before it had started. She was so tired of hurting. Just when everything seemed to be going well, she was dragged back into her turbulent childhood.

"I miscarried three times; then my boyfriend of nine years up and left. He left me in the hospital with a note that said 'I can't do this anymore.' When I got home the following day, he had taken everything but some of my clothes. He even took my cat that he hated."

"What? Why?"

"I think he was trying to make me pay for something that I did to him, but I can't figure out what it was. Or maybe it was that he was just a jerk. If I think of him as a jerk, it's easier to say good riddance."

"What are you doing here?" Sarah asked, still trying to hide her face.

"In the infirmary?"

Sarah nodded.

"I was here getting a lesson on venipuncture when they brought you in. You were in kind of a delirium. Miss Anna gave you a sedative to relax you. They asked me to stay and watch you until they got back or until you woke up."

"Please don't get them just yet. I don't want the dean to see me like this."

"I understand. I can give you a couple minutes."

Sarah nodded in appreciation as Ulyssa dried a few more of Sarah's tears and pulled a chair around to face her.

"For whatever reason," Ulyssa continued, "it wasn't time for me to bring a baby into this world. Maybe it was God's way of saying 'you're not ready yet either.' When I look back and see what type of person I was then and who I am now and who I will be when I leave this place, I can say that I will need a large wall in my house to put up all the 'best mom ever' awards scribbled in crayon."

"You still want to be a mom even after you went through all that?"

"Even if I have to adopt or become a foster mom."

"Why?" Sarah asked.

"For children, it is life at its purest. I want to be a mom who can help them keep that purity as long as possible."

Sarah sighed and grumbled. "Why couldn't my mom be half of who you are?"

"I don't know, Miss Sarah."

"Can you call someone?"

Ulyssa pushed a call button for the PA, then turned back to Sarah. "We all fell down countless times before we learned to walk, and we'll fall down countless times before we learn how to live."

"I'm tired of pulling myself out of the gutter. I finally have something good happen, then I get strapped to a bed and I have to pee."

"Oh my. Can you hold it?"

"Yeah, for about thirty more seconds."

"I'm not allowed to do anything except push the call button and keep you company."

"I thought I was alright but it just kinda hit all of a sudden."

Ulyssa pushed the call button again. "I called them again."

"Why does it, you know, losing the . . ." Sarah paused, not wanting to fall back down that dark hole again, "hurt so much?"

"Because you care."

"Does it go away?"

"No. It doesn't go away. You learn to accept it as part of your life. Part of what makes you, you. It doesn't go away entirely. But you can find reasons why it was not the right time." Sarah looked up into the kind and caring eyes of a future nurse. "I guess you could look forward to Alzheimer's. Then I guess you'd be able to forget it along with everything else and have a better excuse for wetting the bed."

Sarah laughed at the simple joke. "Please. I've got to pee really bad."

"Sorry. I can't. I can get you a bed pan though."

"No. I don't want a bed pan," Sarah huffed, and slumped back into the bed. "What if your child turns out to be a rotten little monster?"

"Then I'll still be there for them, but I won't take any of the blame for their actions nor bail them out of anything."

"What if they turn their back on you completely?"

Ulyssa pondered the question. "I would imagine it would hurt, but I would make sure they know that they can call anytime."

They sat in silence a moment before Ulyssa spoke again. "What if you do everything right and you get to watch them walk across the stage for their college diploma, hold one of their children named after you and share in many wonderful moments? Would it be worth it?"

"I'm just so afraid of screwing up. I don't want to be responsible for a child who grows up to be a monster."

"If you have this much concern, just add a big pot full of love and you'll do just fine. Besides, you always have the call center."

"Call center?"

"Yeah. Some of us are moms and longtime babysitters." Ulyssa wiped a few stray tears from Sarah's face.

Sarah nodded and flashed a smile of appreciation. "Okay. Give me the bed pan. I can't hold it."

"No need." Dean Vickery's voice came from the other side of the curtain. "Unbuckle her. I think she'll be alright now. Ulyssa, are you sure you want to be a phlebotomist? I think you'd make a great counselor."

"Sir, you know I'm a vampire," Ulyssa said, unbuckling the straps.

Chapter XVIII

"No. No. No." Temperance clenched her fists in her hair. "Don't do that!" Temperance panicked as the computer screen froze and reverted back to a default blue screen. Sucking air through her teeth, she pounded on the keyboard, trying to save the first set of tests that her small class had just submitted. She had run the punch cards through to score the tests and the data came back garbled with unrecognizable data.

"What's wrong?" Mackenzie Turnmor asked.

"I don't know." Temperance finally released her hair, though several strands had transferred to her hands with her frustrated grip. "I did like I was supposed to do. I fed the test sheets into the machine. It's supposed to calculate all the right and wrong answers, give a high, low, mean and an average."

"It's alright, Miss Temperance. You did good. You taught us everything that we need to know on that section."

"I just wanted to see how we did as a group." Temperance wiggled the mouse on the desk in a feeble attempt to get the computer to wake up. The screen blazed a disappointing blue light back at her.

THE CLASSROOM

"Miss Temperance?" A student's voice came from the back half of the mobile semitrailer classroom. "Something's wrong with the RCs."

"Oh my god. Can anything else go wrong?" Temperance almost screamed in frustration.

The lights to the mobile classroom flickered and extinguished. Gasps from the eight students echoed through the trailer. Temporarily blinded, each student stood in place for fear of causing anything else to tumble out of harmony.

Several seconds passed before light blasted across the classroom, dwarfing the emergency exit signs. A large round shape overtook the doorway. A thump preceded the white stick that flung its way into the capsule.

"Three steps up, sir," came Rebecca's voice. "Miss Temperance. I have your mentor." Rebecca held the man's arm as he felt for the steps. "One, two, three. There's a bench to your left if you need to sit down, or a chair to the right."

"Oh, thank you darling. Are you available for dinner later? You've been a wonderful help," said the round-bellied man.

"No, sir. I am not. I have class," Rebecca replied.

"Well, can you call me when you don't have any class?"

"Unfortunately for you, sir, I will have class from now until the day I die."

"Well, you sure know how to kill a guy's mood," the round man said.

"Sorry, sir. It's just how they raise us around here." Rebecca steadied him as he stepped into the trailer and the lights flickered back on.

"Damn, can someone turn the lights off. They're hurting my eyes." The man adjusted his permanently dark glasses.

Tabatha, a woman in her late forties who would be graduating soon and was taking the CDL training as a secondary means of income, ran to adjust the lights, then noticed the brilliant white of the cane that he was holding. "Miss Temperance, can you come here, please?"

Temperance came around the partition to see the person attached to the male voice. "Yes sir, can I help you?"

"Well, it's hard for me to see for myself, but I'm looking for a young lady who goes by the name of Lloyd Temperance Kingsetter."

"I am Miss Temperance—" Temperance stopped mid-introduction and stared at the man. "What do you want?" Temperance said, her voice becoming agitated.

"Well, by the tone of your voice I think I'm in the right place."

"Get the flip out of here. You have no business here."

The round man paused a moment. "Sounds like I'm in the right place." The veteran driver cast his cane in an arc. "Where's a chair? I've gotta sit down."

Rebecca led him to a chair and helped him sit down. Settling into the seat, he turned loose of the gas he had been holding in since his arrival at the academy. Groans echoed through the small trailer as the sound reverberated off the bare walls, and the putrid fragrance lofted, attacking the students' noses.

"Why are you here?" Temperance hissed through her clenched teeth.

"I was told you needed a veteran driver. Hell, I know there isn't a damn person here who could teach anyone anything about driving."

****

"We need you to testify against your father," Mr. Henderson said, setting his briefcase on a counter. "Your father is denying all the allegations and threatening to sue for defamation."

"Doesn't the DNA test prove otherwise?" Sarah asked, trying to dodge stepping foot in a courtroom again.

"The DNA test came back inconclusive," the attorney said. "Your mother was our best witness and would have been able to carry the bulk of the argument because she was older and turning evidence for a lighter sentence."

"So, you're not going to be able to nail him?" Sarah sat back in her chair, folding her arms in front of her. "He'll get to walk free?"

"That's why we're here. We need to set up and get a deposition from you. It may be difficult for you, but it needs to be done."

"Why can't the DNA evidence do all this for me?"

"Miss Sarah," Gearda interjected, "is there a reason you don't want to do this?"

"I don't want to relive that nightmare. I blocked it out for a reason. I'm tired of hurting. I'm tired of this cra—" Sarah unclenched her fists. "Of this stuff raining down on me. I just want something good to happen. Someone to believe me."

"Miss Sarah. It would be nice if it were that simple. The problem is that no one knows who you are, and you were convicted of a serious crime; therefore you are stereotyped. It's a steep hill to climb."

Sarah sagged in her chair. Her eyes searched the tiled floor for a secret door she could climb in and hide.

"It's not that it's impossible, just harder," Mr. Henderson reassured her.

Sarah looked up, straightened her posture and cleared her throat. "Okay. What do I need to do?"

"We need to take another DNA sample, and we need to do a video deposition."

"Why does she need to do a video deposition?" Gearda asked.

"Their lawyers want to send it to their psychologists to see if she exhibits any signs of lying."

"Sir. So, they want to basically tear apart my deposition and make me look like I'm making this up." Sarah sat up, trying to be an engaging player in the game and use a cool and even-tempered tone.

"Plainly?—yes. Their job is to discredit you. We want to be very thorough in our steps forward, so that when they try to discredit you, they have next to nothing to substantiate their claim. The judge in the case tends to side with law enforcement but is still a very thorough judge who wants to see every speck of evidence.

"We will have two samples taken from you and sent to two different labs and the results brought in for comparison. The first results did show that you were the mother of the child in question, but the father's DNA didn't match, so we're going to have a representative from our office witness the extraction of DNA and see that it is sent to two different labs."

"And then?" Sarah asked.

"We wait. It could be a few weeks."

Sarah rolled her eyes in frustration.

"Sir!" Temperance burst through the door. "Why is my father here?"

Chapter XIX

Dean Vickery dragged Temperance out of the clinic and into the hallway next to shipping and receiving. Temperance's unpleasant expression matched Dean Vickery's. "Number one, that was extremely rude and uncalled for. I know that you know better. You wouldn't want me to barge in on one of your classes and tell you what an inconsiderate little snot you're being, would you?"

"No, sir." Temperance retreated half a step, her shoulders slumped.

"You spoke so highly of him that I automatically assumed that he would be a good fit to help you teach your class. I apologize for not consulting with you, but all the other candidates weren't a good match. He has over thirty years of experience in many different driving situations, and from others, I've heard that he's one of the most skilled drivers in the country.

"That is the reason I asked him to join us. He can teach you and your class more than any driving school in the nation could."

"But sir, how can he teach if he's blind?" Temperance's tone mellowed, yet she still sought a reason not to work with him.

"Just like you teach without a degree or experience."

"Sir?"

"With passion and drive. It sounds like you need to patch a few things up in your relationship with him anyway. You're stuck with him no matter what. We don't have the budget to find a replacement, and the rest home said that he wasn't welcome back."

Temperance's eyes widened as she looked up at the dean. "Why?"

"Well, basically he doesn't play well with others. The bank foreclosed on his house and his savings is nonexistent. He won't file for disability. He keeps trying to wander off. Claims that he isn't useful to anyone—that everyone should just let him die.

"So, whatever it is that has you bent out of shape about your father, you need to suck it up and deal with it like a good manager. A good manager gets talented people to do amazing things, even if they are . . . a-holes."

"Yes, sir."

"So, don't be an a-hole, put your game face on and get back to work."

"Sir, he farted in the trailer and we had to evacuate it due to the odor."

"Then get a can of spray."

Temperance grumbled under her breath, pausing to look for any other way to dodge the situation. With a miniature foot stomp, she caved to the dean's suggestions. "Yes, sir," Temperance said, then turned to the supply counter. "Miss Rebecca. I need a can of air freshener. My classroom got contaminated."

****

"It's not worth it," Sarah complained as she swung her legs over the edge of the hospital bed. "He'll just get probation at the most, and none of his cronies will penalize any misbehavior. What kind of justice is that?"

"We need to do the right thing," Mr. Henderson said, loosening his blue tie.

"This is a school of business. So, one of the lessons that I learned is that sometimes you have to cut your losses. Is it worth bringing back up everything that I locked away? What do I have to gain if I have to relive all those nightmares over and over again just to see him get a slap on the wrist?"

"Look, we're on your side." Mr. Henderson pinched his brow, seeming to fight off a headache. "We wouldn't want to pursue this unless we know that we can see justice being served. We want to see this guy put away for a very long time, but we need your help to do it."

Sarah groaned at the request, then sighed. "What do you need me to do?"

"Like I said earlier, we need to do another DNA test. We're going to send it to two different labs. Tomorrow, we'll do the deposition. Miss Gearda . . ." The attorney turned toward the counselor. "It's 'Gearda,' right?"

"Yes."

"Miss Gearda will be in the next room listening, so that afterward, you and Miss Gearda can talk about anything that you need to."

Sarah nodded. "Yes, sir. Anything else, sir?"

"Not that we anticipate. When we get the DNA results back, we should be able to seal everything up. I don't see any reason that it should go to trial."

****

A dozen eyes stared at Temperance's determined face as she marched straight for the mobile classroom door. Twisting the cap off of the spray can, she handed it to a student, then grabbed for the door handle while pressing the button atop the can of highly fragrant lavender mist. Sweeping the can back and forth like a fire extinguisher battling flames, she covered the entire trailer in a fog of fragrance.

Returning to the man holding a white cane, she looked down on him, fretting over how to handle the disgusting lump that continually denied that he was her father. Gripping the can, she let instinct take over. Lifting the can high over her head, she activated the button to empty the remaining contents above his head.

"God dammit. What the hell are you doing?" Harris said, flailing his hands about, trying to block the lavender mist raining down on him. He picked up his cane and flung it at Temperance, smacking her across the hand.

"Ow! Flippin' heck. Why do you have to be so dang mean?" Temperance shook off the sting.

"It's my defense mechanism. Keeps everybody away," Harris growled.

Temperance continued unloading the can above his head. Harris gripped his cane and swung harder at his daughter, slamming the white stick into her middle. Jerking it back, he lost his grip as Temperance trapped the cane against her body and twisted it out of his grasp. She tossed the cane to the far side of the classroom and finished emptying the lavender scent onto him.

"If you want to play, old man, I can match you trick for trick."

The door was still open and the rest of the class stood outside snickering. Temperance stormed to the only two windows toward the front of the trailer and opened them up to circulate the foul-now-flowery air out and let breathable air in. Harris sat with a smug look on his face, grumbling to himself.

"Alright class, come back in." Temperance went around the room straightening chairs and setting remote controls back on the shelves and placing the RC trucks back in their designated spots.

"How can you be a truck driver if you can't even cuss?"

"Old man, you just wait until I get out of here. I'll show you how to cuss. Until then, I'm going to behave myself *and* you're going to behave yourself or you're gonna be slapped in a nursing home so dang fast that . . ." Temperance paused, searching for words.

"Can't even speak, neither."

Temperance fumed. Grabbing Harris's white cane, she tossed it at him and turned to the front of the class.

"Since the computer crashed, I'll have to grade your tests by hand. So, why don't you start reading through chapter two, then we'll—"

"Hey!" a student screeched as she jumped out of her seat, spinning to face Harris's grin. His cane was still stretched out with the end sitting atop the student's seat.

Temperance glared at her father, waiting for an explanation.

"I wanted to see if she was wet. Ready to be bred."

"You want someone who's wet, old man?"

Harris gave a gruff chuckle of satisfaction that someone understood him and the hint of an idea that he might get what he wanted.

Temperance stormed out of the trailer. Her class stood wide-eyed and whispering that she was going to get the dean and have him removed from the property. Harris sat in his chair, leaning on his cane and looking satisfied with his actions.

"Cover the computers!" Teresa said, charging forward with her CDL book and opening it at its stapled center. Students scrambled, charging one way or another as the first blast of water spattered through the open door.

Temperance stepped up into the trailer and pulled at the garden hose. The hose ripped across the lawn and uprooted a few flowers that had just been planted. Her death grip on the spray nozzle dodged the flailing cane trying in earnest to dislodge her fingers from the trigger.

"God dammit. Cut that—" Harris's rant was cut short by a stream of water hammering his face.

"You wanted to feel if someone was wet. Well, you better get to feeling. I don't think you'll be disappointed now!" Temperance screamed at the vision-impaired lump. Water flooded the floor as students picked up anything that might get wet in the monsoon.

Releasing the grip on the spray nozzle, Temperance stood back, watching to see if he was deserving of a second round. Harris pulled his dark glasses off his face and wiped the water from his eyes. The long moment screamed for something, yet she could only hear the drops of water landing in the growing lake.

"What the heck, Lloyd?" Harris Kingsetter kept his head cast down to his lap. Temperance paused a beat before flinging the hose back outside. Going to the closet in the corner, she reached for a broom to sweep the water out the door when Harris roared with laughter.

"What the heck are you laughing at?" Temperance demanded. Harris continued to laugh at the expense of the naive wannabe drivers. Temperance made a break for the door, intent on seeing her father escorted from the property.

"Sit down, girl," Harris said.

Temperance continued toward the door.

"I said sit down!" Harris barked, standing to block the door.

The tone of his voice gave Temperance pause. She hesitated right before her father, debating if she should push by him or sit and listen. She continued forward to go and reason with the dean.

"I said sit down," Harris growled at her. "You're about to learn something."

Temperance stopped dead in her tracks. It wasn't her father's words but her father's attitude that had changed. That was what scared her into submission.

"Sit down, LT." Harris pulled her pet name from the nearly nonexistent vocabulary that she once knew from him. Turning his head, he watched out of the corner of his eye to see if everyone had settled down to listen. He had been told that his right eye had turned completely white, but he could see fragments of images with the peripheral vision of his left eye.

"What's the first thing that's going to happen when you walk in to apply for a job?" Harris said in a conversational tone. He blankly stared at the floor, waiting for anyone to answer.

Kimberly, a young adult who was nearing her scheduled flight out of the academy, spoke up, "You show them your resume and credentials."

"Fucking schoolbook answer." Harris turned his head to see what he could of the class he was to help teach. "That's a goddamn worthless answer. You think that's the first thing that happens. Damn, you girls are stupid. If that's what you think, fucking go home and play with your dolls.

"You're not wanted in this world. This is a man's world. Go find a goddamn knitting job." Harris paused and looked back at the black void that continually thwarted him, telling him that he was worthless. "You're going to be judged as soon as you walk through that door. That fucking piece of paper that you're fixin' to hand them is already in the trash. They're going to judge you because you're a girl, and if you wear makeup, you just as well find a pole to dance on.

"Companies need shit hauled and they want men to get it done for them. There ain't any makeup in the world that'll drive a truck down the road.

"Besides, if you wear makeup, they'll think that you'll spend more time looking in the mirror than at the road, and that's how you get people killed. You're in control of a forty-ton battering ram. There's no time to have a goddamn breakdown over a broken nail.

"Fucking woman driver was doing her makeup in the mirror when she should have been driving. She drifted into the other lane—semi driver hit his brakes on ice, the car turned, and the truck ran over the back half of the car. I watched the whole damn thing. Kid's head popped off and went rolling down the street. Both the semi driver and her are still in the mental ward.

"Your damn nail polish ain't gonna help ya there."

Chapter XX

"What do you mean, the DNA doesn't match?" Sarah hissed at the attorney. The hearing to present evidence for trial was fast approaching. Sarah squirmed in her seat. Gearda had taken her usual place behind her desk, but turned sideways to view Sarah, Dean Vickery and the attorney.

"Your DNA matches perfectly with everything." The attorney avoided using 'daughter' after witnessing Sarah's meltdown a few weeks before. "Somehow Mr. Menendez's DNA doesn't. Both labs provided identical results. I don't understand it either. Your testimony is going to be essential to show what kind of man he is. Outside the home he has a sparkling clean record. Everything he has done seems to be golden."

"It was far from golden for me," Sarah huffed.

"It may be an uphill battle, and Mr. Menendez has threatened to file defamation charges in retaliation," Mr. Henderson warned.

"Shhh . . ." Sarah paused to regroup and restrain herself from the use of profanity. "What are our options?"

"Well, if we give up now, we're likely to face defamation charges but can downplay them a little—get them reduced or maybe dropped. With Mr. Menendez just starting his term of office, he isn't going to let this go. His integrity is in question and he wants his outward appearance to be pristine."

Sarah shook her head in frustration. "I'm not lying about this. This is what he did to me for four years. Almost every night I had to endure him rutting on me. My own father. How could anyone do that?"

"I've heard that question before and the answers vary widely." Mr. Henderson shifted his weight from one foot to the other, pushed off the wall he was leaning against and walked in a small circle, rubbing his chin. He turned back to Sarah after searching and failing to find a different way to say what he was about to. "We found out something else."

"Great," Sarah scoffed and rolled her eyes. "You're gonna tell me he's not my father or I have a dozen siblings waiting to find me."

The attorney paused a little too long.

Sarah sat a little straighter in her chair. "What? What is it?"

"Well, yes, and we don't know."

Sarah blinked at the sudden information. "What the heck do you mean, 'yes and we don't know'?"

"Yes, in that he is not your biological father, which leaves the door wide open about who is and if or how many siblings you have."

"You're shitting me, right?" Sarah's voice sharpened. She started to shove herself out of the chair, then thought better of it and forced her emotions not to control her actions.

"Sarah! I understand that this comes as a surprise, but you still have to maintain control," Gearda reprimanded. She glared at Sarah after silently exhaling.

"Sorry, Miss Gearda. I had to blow off a little steam. I didn't want to keep it bottled and make something worse later." Sarah pulled the half-hearted excuse out to justify her actions. She looked back to the attorney. "So, you're sure he's not my father?"

The attorney nodded.

"Good. I don't have to admit that I'm related to that—"

Gearda drew a breath in and held it while beaming her eyes at Sarah to remain professional.

Sarah paused to search for an appropriate word that didn't defy the academy's policy. "Rectum. Miss Gearda, anyone who does that doesn't deserve all the luxuries that he's been afforded. Heck, he doesn't even deserve how well the prison systems treat the average inmate. My only hope is that he gets thrown in with a bunch of brothers. Then justice would seem a bit more fair in my book."

"We understand how you feel. We can't make an individual prison for each inmate to cater to all the varying degrees of crime," Gearda lectured.

"I know, Miss Gearda. I guess that the minimum that I want is that my story is told and that I am believed."

"I can see that your story is told in court, but I can't guarantee that everyone will believe you," Mr. Henderson said.

"I just want someone of authority above him to believe in me. Of course, I'd like him to go to jail, but without a DNA match I understand that it will be near impossible."

"Do you want to move forward then?" Mr. Henderson asked.

"Yes, sir."

Chapter XXI

To wear anything but scrubs, fatigues or a stiff business suit was the most glorious thing Jamika could think of. Her free-flowing knee-length dress contrasted her ebony skin. The white ruffles loosely caressed her arms as a sprinkle of silver glitter reflected the imitation firelight in the intimate dining theater.

"This is beautiful. How did you do all this?" Jamika waved a hand at their surroundings.

Landon scribbled out a quick message, then slid it across the table.

Dean Vickery had arranged to meet Landon for lunch a few days after he clued Jamika in on what Landon had tried to ask her. During that lunch, Dean Vickery grilled Landon like any protective father would over his daughter. Landon replied with many "Yes, sirs" and "No, sirs" to all the essential questions as if he were to have his manhood removed if he had even the slightest thought of any of Dean Vickery's daughters.

Dean Vickery didn't have daughters though. He had five sons who had all left the nest and left him to face a mountain of estrogen seemingly by himself. He thought of these women as his children, like a teacher thought of her class as her children. He did all that he could to fill the shoes of the responsible parent that so many didn't have.

You will have to ask Dean Vickery. If I have to explain how I did all this, I would get writer's cramp and our night would be over too soon, Landon's note said.

Jamika smiled, remembering how Dean Vickery had walked her out to the waiting limo. Landon hadn't been able to scribble a word. He stared dumbfoundedly at Jamika in her white dress with a row of modest ruffles across the top to match the flowing ruffles swishing across her knees. Dean Vickery told him to have her back by eleven. When he nodded in agreement, Dean Vickery produced a set of handcuffs and handcuffed Jamika and Landon together.

Landon pulled the note tablet back and scribbled some more as they waited for their food to be delivered. *I like how you closed the handcuff back around your wrist after I unlocked it with the key Dean Vickery gave me.*

Jamika melted. She saw that Dean Vickery wanted her to have a special night and added a few touches of his own to make it special.

The food arrived and they took turns helping each other, as they each needed two hands to cut the shrimp on her plate and the steak on his. As they worked together with her left hand holding the delicacies with a fork and his right hand cutting them, their cuffed hands had their own conversation, caressing each other's fingers as the gleaming pair of handcuffs reminded them of their inseparability.

"What else do you have planned for our date?" Jamika asked, sampling the shrimp from the academy-run restaurant. It was the only place that Dean Vickery would allow the two of them to go, according to the bylaws of the school.

Movie.

"If we have to be back by eleven, we won't have time for a two-hour movie," Jamika said, voicing her concern.

Landon scribbled on his pad again and slid it around for her to read. *Don't worry. The film is only 30 minutes.*

Jamika smiled. She yearned to be the bad girl and extend their evening, but respected that he was one hundred and ten percent gentleman and let him perform to his utmost gentlemanly persuasion. Though the conversation between them was minimal, the energy between the two could be felt by anyone walking by.

Through the dismal end of thermodynamics and aroma, Jamika and Landon continued to enjoy the challenge of helping each other with their meals as one. It took several attempts to learn how and when the other needed a second hand to assist with cutting or scooping food onto a fork or spoon, or holding a tray so the other could cut off a slice of butter. Operating the peppercorn grinder was the trickiest part of their evening—it was dropped or accidentally slammed into their food three different times before they gave up.

They moved from the dining table to the small lawn outside the restaurant, where Landon had brought in his own leather couch that they could watch the film from. He had downloaded it onto his phone and he played it through a projector against the white wall of the restaurant. As they settled in on the couch after a brief restroom break, Jamika closed the handcuff back around her wrist and rested against Landon to enjoy the show.

****

"I love the movie that you picked," Jamika whispered in Landon's ear as the limousine pulled away from the restaurant.

I wanted to express how I felt about you. I am not part of the LDS community, but I definitely agree with how they portray the value of a wife in this film. As I delivered more and more packages to the academy, I saw your confidence and your sadness. I knew that if your happiness, determination and forgiveness could match your confidence, then I believe Dean Vickery might find himself in the ranching business.

Jamika had no words. She snuggled into his arm, shoulder and chest until the limousine ride concluded in front of the academy. Dean Vickery met them at the door. Landon grudgingly pulled the handcuff key from his pocket, unlocked the handcuffs and placed them in Dean Vickery's hand. After one long, final hug with Landon, Jamika took Dean Vickery's arm as he escorted her back into the building. She smiled and whispered a quiet thank you to the dean, as the handcuffs had been the most beautiful part of her evening, binding her to the one person that made her feel complete.

Chapter XXII

D o you swear to tell the whole truth and nothing but the truth, so help you?" the bailiff asked Sarah Menendez.
"Yes."

"Please state your full legal name," Mr. Henderson said.

"Sarah Montoya Menendez," Sarah said confidently.

"Are you Michael Menendez's biological child?" asked her attorney.

"No, sir."

"Can you elaborate?" Mr. Henderson continued.

"My mother had told me that he was my father. Due to recent testing I was told that I was not." Sarah shifted in the witness stand, trying and failing to be more comfortable with her surroundings.

"What was it that made you understand this?" Mr. Henderson asked.

"The DNA test that I recently took to double confirm who my biological parents were," Sarah said.

"And have you been told the results of this test?"

"Yes, sir. From what I was told, they were inconclusive, yet showed me as the mother of the child. From the second set of tests, I was told that the two different labs found that I was the mother of the child. Michael's DNA did not match the paternal side of mine or my child's DNA, as per the tests."

"So, until recently, you viewed Mr. Menendez as your biological father?" Mr. Henderson shifted slowly from one foot to the other while occasionally glancing at his notes.

"Yes."

"You viewed him as someone who was supposed to nurture and support you as you grew?"

"Yes."

"Was he a decent father at any time when you were still living with him?"

"Yes."

"What kind of things did he do?" her lawyer asked, working to extract all the necessary information to paint the full spectrum of the man sitting behind the defense table.

Sarah stared at her hands, wishing she didn't have to say the slightest thing positive about her father. "He would take me to the park and let me play, but he wouldn't participate."

"What do you mean by not participate?"

"He would sit on the bench and watch or talk with some of the other parents."

"Did he take you anywhere else?"

"Not that I remember."

"What about home life? What did he do when both of you were home?"

Sarah glanced at her father, sitting at the defendant's table. He seemed indifferent to any of the proceedings going on around him. The quaking little girl inside gave way to the tickle of anger that had built since she realized that she was not to blame like she had first been told. Months at the academy had taught her to control her anger and that it could be used as a tool when directed properly. Here she used it like a knife made of words to sever forever the man's title as her father.

"He watched TV or a ball game," Sarah continued.

"Where were you, usually, when he was watching TV?"

"I was usually in a corner playing with my toys."

"Did he ever have you do anything?"

"He had me make his drink for him, so he didn't have to miss any part of a ball game."

"What kind of drink do you remember making?"

"Gin and tonic."

"Did you think that this was odd?"

"No."

"Did he teach you anything? Anything like life skills? How to check the oil in your car? How to change a tire?"

"He taught me how to make a gin and tonic."

"Is there anything else he taught you?"

Sarah pulled at the sleeve of the orange jumpsuit she wore. Because she had to be transferred back to her hometown for the trial, she had to stay at the county jail and be booked in all over again. When she'd first filled out the application for the academy, she hadn't realized what an opportunity it had presented her. She was happy now that they had selected her and allowed her to turn her life around.

"He taught me how to be resourceful, to think on my feet." Sarah looked at her father, wearing a gray business suit, and began talking straight at him. "He taught me how to fend for myself and to only depend on myself. He taught me that I could take from people whatever I wanted and not feel guilty. He taught me to fight anyone wearing a badge or anyone that threatened my lifestyle."

"Aside from putting a roof over your head and meals on the table, did he do anything else?"

"Aside from arguing with my mother, no I can't think of much else."

"Do you remember when things changed, when he started attacking you?"

Sarah returned her stare to the empty space a few feet in front of her. She wanted to go into that vacuum that Gearda had taught her to seek refuge in, where she could get everything out without falling to pieces in the middle of it. It was a preselected imaginary cocoon that kept outside influences away and inside influences in a numb and neutral voice. She reminded herself that she could fall apart after, but not during. "I remember hiding in my room. My mother and him were yelling for what seemed like hours. I tried to cover my ears with pillows, but I could still hear them."

"How old were you when this happened?"

"I was ten years old."

"Could you hear what they were saying?"

"Nothing other than a few cuss words. I don't remember much. It was all really muffled."

"What happened next?"

"I heard a thud, like something heavy hit the wall. It was quiet for a little while, then the yelling resumed. My bedroom door crashed open. Before I knew it, he was on top of me."

"Where was your mother?"

"She was there shortly after, trying to console me and telling me that it would be over soon. That I just needed to lay still and it would be over faster."

"Did you know what was about to happen?"

"No. I clung to my mother's hand, trying not to move, trusting that if I did what she said, things wouldn't be worse."

"What happened next?"

"He pulled my pajamas down and entered me."

Chapter XXIII

Sarah pulled a towel off the shelf and stepped out of the shower. The timer had run out, defaulting to the typical cold water that ran through every other faucet. The trickle of water had caused her to shiver as she hastily tried to rinse the rest of the soap off her body. The extended stay in the shower couldn't wash the cringey slime that seemed to encase her skin. It didn't wash away the hate and contempt she held for her father. If she stood under Niagara Falls, she still wouldn't feel that that tarnish could be stripped from her and carried downriver to a forgotten ocean.

To be forced to relive the four years of abuse, she hoped the judge would see fit to impose more than a slap on the wrist. The thoughts wrenched at her mind, driving her to insanity. She had to bring herself back to the present and to the future. She struggled to put it out of her mind and focused on the jail-issue garments lying on the bench.

The generic underclothes pulled at her skin, agitating a new red mark around her neck. Little things added up to a mountain when she compared what she had before at the academy to what she had in the jail. Though she didn't really own anything material, she owned something much more valuable. She owned her self-worth. Something that no one could take from her. Going back to the county jail was almost a trial in and of itself—a trial by light of reflection.

"You changed." A voice startled her as she put a set of her assigned clothes in the laundry hamper. Sarah turned to find an older woman standing before her. She didn't recognize the face, but she did recognize the scar on the woman's hand. The motherly figure, at least motherly in the way that Sarah had become accustomed to, was one of her mother's chain-smoking friends from the trailer park—the loud, belligerent woman who cussed worse than a sailor and bragged continuously how she still had one tooth.

"Maj the Badge." Sarah smiled.

"I can't hug ya or I gets in trouble," Maj said. "Or I be squeezin' da fucking crap out ya."

"What do you mean changed?" Sarah asked.

"Yer not da frightened little plump girl who hid under meh kitchen table, nor you da mean woman who jumped to a fight if she was rit or wrong."

Sarah didn't know what to say. Her life in that trailer park seemed like someone else's life now. It was like some past episode of *Jerry Springer*, where turmoil was the heartbeat of the trailer park.

Constant bickering enveloped the neighborhood and became a staple of life. The mayor was quoted saying, "That type of activity is going to happen, and as such, it's our job to keep it contained to an isolated area. If the area and people are disrupted, their less than desirable activities will then be dispersed throughout the community." He had called for the police chief and investigators not to press the area too hard to prevent their lifestyle from spilling out to the rest of the city.

Sarah was starting to see the genius behind some community leaders. How one would never be able to get rid of the "bad element" in any community because that bad element was a continued generational factor. The mayor preferred to isolate them like a tank full of betta fish and watch as they destroyed themselves. If the decent folks of that area wanted them out, they would have to either come up with a clever way of causing the drug dealer or other nuisance to move, or start their own neighborhood watch.

But nothing could make a criminal stop being a criminal except a willingness to mind all the rules and laws. She understood now what they meant by always moving forward. Where someone was going was more important than where they'd been.

"Wh't ya doin' back h're?" Maj asked. "I tought you off t' 'nother instution." She sought any gossip she could find and spread it in a way that she thought would benefit her own interests.

"I have a court thing that I have to attend," Sarah said, trying to sound indifferent. She didn't know what anyone else knew or the consequences if she were to reveal anything about her case. She just wanted to quietly get the whole thing over with so she could get on with her life. Besides, her lawyer and Miss Gearda advised her to not say a thing, to keep her cards close to her chest.

"I heared dat you so-called father git locked up. Big news, all over da city 'n' a spot on da state news."

"Oh yeah?"

"Yup. Rumor is dat he molested some child back in the day. I tought it be for 'is under-table deals—all da shady deals he be part of. If yer back here during dis trial, I say da first part true."

Sarah stared blankly at her mother's friend.

172

"Lawyer got yer lip zipped?"

"Yes."

"Good. Best you don't say anything, but it'd be a damn good idea ta keep yer ears clean—and your nose for that matter. Ya never know what ya hear in a rumor mill. Rumors have da way of being true."

"Thanks, Maj. I planned on keeping to myself anyway. What time is lights out?"

"'N bout 'n' hour. How long're ya here fer?"

"I don't know. I feel like the square peg being slammed into a round hole."

"Welcome 'ome, kiddo."

Sarah gave half a smile. The thought that this was her home upset her. Good memories invaded her mind, filling an empty void. A need to belong and have roots. Maj and her other neighbors in the park had roots, though some of them had rotten roots. But they were still roots, and roots were something that she didn't have.

"Home." Sarah gave a slight huff at the idea.

Sarah lay on her bunk and stared at the ceiling just a few feet in front of her face. "Why am I doing this?" Sarah whispered. "Why am I reliving this nightmare for no apparent reason? There's nothing to gain by doing this." She lay in silence for a moment before continuing. "God, damn you, are you listening? I'm trying to do the right thing here. Is it so horrible to do the right thing that I can't catch a break? Did I commit a horrible crime to wish my parents dead? I did wish that at times, but most of the time, I just wanted them to be normal.

"I wanted to be someone they could be proud of, but they used me for their own selfish benefit. Please let what I'm doing be valuable to me or even anyone but me. I don't care. I just want to see justice served.

"Please let me understand that you're trying, and that maybe I need a little more patience." Sarah pulled her blanket up over her shoulders and drifted off.

Maj contemplated her words, as she was on the bunk underneath Sarah. She had known Sarah since she was fourteen, and praying was something that she never did. Maj heard most of her words and now lay awake thinking of a solution. One that contradicted her selfish reasoning.

Chapter XXIV

Something botherin' ya?" Maj called to Sarah as she sat around the common room waiting for one fate or the other. "Come sit down. Tell meh sometin'."

Maj was like the matriarch of the trailer court, which apparently spread to the county jail. She knew many of the faces in the jail and received a general respect among the inmates. Her name was Majorine but she'd "smack you stupid" if you ever tried to call her that. Sarah had seen her rip an officer up one side and down the other for calling her by her birth name, and a judge that continued to call her that when she asked him not to ended up resigning and moving away a short time later. Maj was said to practice voodoo from time to time. Most people left her alone; therefore, Sarah assumed that something big must have happened if the police had to root her out of the trailer park.

Sarah had emptied her tray and started back to her bunk. No one was in the four-bunk room, and Sarah wanted to resume her normal routine as much as possible. She had slept through until breakfast, missing the morning exercises that she used to do back at the academy.

"Tell meh sometin' good. God knows you been t'rough hell already," Maj said.

After saying her prayer the night before, Sarah had stared at the ceiling until she drifted off. She wondered why she was remarkably calm when she thought she would be agitated. Now Maj had summoned her to sit and tell her something good. She wondered how she could say anything good when the process—her intellectual growth process—wasn't complete. Plus, she wasn't sure if she should say anything about the academy or the wonderful benefits it had.

"No. I just feel . . . I don't know, out of place."

"Darlin,' we all outta place here. Dat why 'm here. Kep 'em all in line."

Sarah smiled at her lie. "Come on now, Maj, that's not why you're here."

"Looks at you, speakin' proper English 'n' all. Whateva got into you?"

Sarah sighed. "Understanding. Understanding that my life is my own and I don't have to live by anyone else's standards except my own."

Maj eyeballed her friend's daughter, evaluating the authenticity of what she said. "Bullshit."

"Maj. I'm not going to sit here and be questioned if what I say is true or not. If you don't think I'm good company anymore—"

"Oh, sit down. Dat's not what I mean." Maj smacked the table a couple times and looked at Sarah. "Wh't y' been doing dat's be causin' dis damn change?"

"I'm not allowed to say." Sarah sat back down and stiffened her resolve to protect the people and institution that helped her see the type of person she wanted to become.

"Well damn, girl. I'm tryin' t' make conversation wit' ya. Find out what ya been drinkin' ta make ya all uppity. Yer panties in a twist or somepin'?"

"No, I just don't feel comfortable about saying where I've been or what I've been doing. Yes, I know I've changed, but I don't know if it's good or bad. I just don't want to talk about the aspects that have changed me."

"See! Dat what'm talkin' 'bout rrt there. Not a cuss word one and usin' 'aspects' instead of 'shit' or 'stuff.' Ya shurz-hell don't fit in 'round her no more."

Sarah started to get up, ready to leave before another insult bloomed from the overly opinionated woman.

"Oh, sit back down. I'll shut up in a minute. Jus' got a couple more thing I need ta say."

Sarah settled back onto the metal bench.

"Whateva 'appen t' ya t' create dis creature dat's sittin' 'nside meh adopted niece's body, I hope dey never turn loose. 'T-ever caused ya t' change, you hold onta dat and run like hell as far away from h're as ya can git." Maj raised her voice to emphasize her next concern. "If I ever find out dat yer livin' in a goddamn trailer park, 'm gonna hunt ya down 'n' kick yer ass. Ya hear me?"

"Yes, ma'am. No more trailer parks for me." Sarah breathed a sigh of relief that the one person she felt semiclose to growing up was on her side as well.

"After ya leave here, I don't want t' ever see ya again."

"Yes, ma'am."

"Yer too damn good fer dis town no more."

"Yes, ma'am."

"Whenever ya git done wherever yer at, I don't want any damn phone calls. I don't want t' see yer face. I jist want ya t' send me a Christmas card once a year to let me know yer alive."

"Yes, ma'am." Sarah smiled.

"Now. I know yer tight-lipped 'bout what ya been doing. I gots some in-fer-mation y'might want t' know. Yer mom and me, we plenty close. She told me thet yer father may not be yers. She asked me to tell ya after she died. Now she dead, so I k'n tell ya now."

"Why didn't you tell me before?"

"Wudn't my secret ta tell."

"Oh."

"Now. Sometin' else that's b'n botherin' me."

Sarah leaned in a little closer.

"Shortly after yer father was arrested, someone broke inta yer house. Trashed the whole damn thing. Yer old boyfriend, he's shacked up with another girl now, he made her go stay at a friend's house before he called the police. She only fifteen, a runaway, so not too good t' be hangin' on the arm of a child.

"Da police come, took photos, filled out some paperwork and handed a card to Jim, the landlord. Dey walked over everyt'n, den left. After dey left, I shuffled through da mess. Dey broke the few pictures of you dat yer mom framed. Other pictures were left unbroken. I saved da photos. I ask Gill, yer boyfriend, if I could keep 'em safe for ya. He complained at first, so I gave 'im a talkin' ta and he come 'round t' my way of t'inkin.'

"Send me dat first Christmas card an' I'll send ya what's yours."

"Yes, ma'am. I'd like that."

"No use kept da trailer. I found da title. I say sign it over t' Jim an' he can do with it what he wants."

"I'll let my lawyer know to look for it. How did you end up in here?"

"Let Shelby barr'er da car. She ran up some parkin' tickets, den wouldn't come bail meh out. I don't give a damn.

178

’Cept fer dat new carton a smokes I bought. I’m sure she’s got ’em smoked up by now.”

“What did you tell the judge?”

“Told da judge dat I didn’t do it. Told ’im dat I be ’appy to sit here ‘n’ let the taxpayers feed meh. Told ’im dat whenever he did catch up dat daughter of mine, t’ make ’er pay fer da smokes she stole fr’m meh.

“He said dat since it’us my car, I be responsible, ‘n’ dat I had to pay. I ass’t him how he going t’ get da money. He slap me wit’ a contempt of court charge. Then ass’t me again. I told him dat I had no money t’ spare to pay dem tickets. Everything I had ’uz to pay rent, utilities, food, car insurance and gas. I’d nothing left.

“Den he ass’t me ’bout my cigarettes. Dat if I could buy cigarettes den I could spare some money t’ pay da ticket. I told him dat I didn’t commit da crime and wasn’t responsible for da tickets. Den I pointed out dat me smoking cigarettes was my gift to the government.”

“Why did you say that?” Sarah asked.

“It blew his mind too. I told ’im dat if I stopped smoking, I live ’bout five year longer. Five year at twelve hundred dollar was seventy dousand dollars dat I be saving the government.”

Sarah chuckled to herself, imagining Maj, in her own way, ripping that judge up one side and down the other.

“He call da prosecuting attorney t’ look see if dey’s any surveillance footage of someone other dan me parking the car.”

“When do you go back?”

“Pert’ soon. I know dey get tired of meh mouth. Most deez cops know dat I fess up if caught too. I don’t give two shits what dey do. I can bounce with da best of dem.”

Chapter XXV

Sarah quietly did her morning exercises just like she'd been doing for months. It had been three days since she talked to Maj. She didn't say anything and kept to herself—just within earshot of potentially good conversations. Most were those of the basic run-of-the-mill infidelity, who didn't come see their kid last weekend, worry over the possibility of losing a job. But there was one bit that interested her.

Sitting down at a table in the common room, she heard a woman complain about a man denying that he was the father. She had gone to confront him about their one-night stand, and he had her arrested for criminal trespassing.

"Dat guy she talk about?" Maj said, setting herself down opposite of Sarah. "Dat yer father."

"Really?"

"Yup. She 'n' him had a little one-night fling. Nine month later, she pop out a kid. She swear up 'n' down he's da father. Never been wit' anyone else."

"I feel her pain. I just want someone to believe that what I say is true. Do you know what I mean?"

"Long time 'go, I want something like dat. As da year go by, I say fuck dat. I only have to please myself. Figure I best focus on dat, since I have t' live wit' myself twenty-four seven."

"I feel for her," Sarah said, glancing at the flustered woman. "I wish I knew something that could help her."

"Tell yer lawyer. If yer lawyer's worth half a shit, he'll look into it." Maj turned to the woman chatting at the next table. "Steph! Steph O'Conner."

The woman with brown pixie-cut hair looked up. Maj waved her over.

"Steph, dis Sarah." The two women nodded to each other. "Sarah can't say anytin' 'cause she's under contract no speak, which make her good listener. Now, I bet meh last tooth dat given a chance, you two be takin' a baseball bat t' da same man."

Sarah looked into the attractive eyes of the young woman. She saw a flash of fire ignite across them. She also saw the same pain and frustration that she saw in the mirror. The same "knowing that you're right, but not knowing how to prove it" look.

"So, you're dealing with the same sphincter that I am?" Stephanie asked.

Sarah let out an exaggerated, frustrated sigh. A lot could be said without voicing a single word.

"He was a charmer," Stephanie continued. "I was a few months out of a bad relationship—wanted to get back in. He said all the right things and I thought he would be fun to be around. I was on the pill, but something happened. After that one night, he never called me. I tried calling him, but it was a disconnected number.

"I let it go and moved on until I found out I was pregnant. So, I tracked him down, found out who he really was and that he was married. He told me to leave before I had a chance to explain why I was there. I tried to argue but he kept cutting me off and threatened to call the police. Within seconds a car pulled up. The officer advised that I leave.

"When I left, I looked at his car and noticed that it was an unmarked police car. From my own car I saw him and the cop chatting it up."

"The cop and your kid's father?" Sarah asked.

"Yes."

Sarah nodded and let Stephanie continue.

"A few days later, I was issued a no trespass order. That was the last I cared to see him. If he was going to be like that, my son would be better off guessing who his daddy was."

"How long ago was that?" Sarah asked.

"Five years."

"So, why are you in here now?"

"My son has something wrong that the doctors can't identify. So, they asked about his father and if I could get some of his medical history to help solve what might be happening. I had forgotten about the no trespass order, which somehow kept getting renewed even though I hadn't tried to contact him in years.

"He changed his phone number but not his address. I walked right up to his door and knocked. He didn't even open the door. The next thing I know, I'm in handcuffs and sitting in the back of a squad car. A tow truck was there in near-record time and towed my car. Now I'm here waiting for a public defender to be assigned to me," Stephanie said, trying to control her anger.

"Who has your son?" Sarah asked.

"My mom. She isn't a confrontational person, but I know she'll take care of Lewis and not let anything happen to him."

"Wow," Sarah said, surprised. "For starters, I'd say that is extremely rude, at a minimum."

"Fuckin' bar minimum," Maj interjected.

"So, you're positive that there couldn't be any other man?" Sarah asked.

"I know I was drinking but stopped an hour before we left the bar; then we ate, then went to his hotel. I felt a little of the alcohol but I was far from sloshed."

"Your name is Stephanie O'Conner?" Sarah wanted to voice the name to help imprint it in her mind.

"O'Conner!" a voiced boomed across the room.

Stephanie stood. "Yes, sir?"

"You're being moved," replied the booming voice again.

Stephanie looked back down at Sarah and quietly said, "I know there's at least two other women in town that are like me."

Sarah nodded in understanding. Stephanie's hushed tone made the hair stand on the back of her neck like some unseen evil was about to strike. The atmosphere also seemed to suddenly change with a charged, invisible tension. The women carried on their usual conversations but shifted to an edginess, like they were being watched. Sarah knew that the cameras were watching and recording, but somehow she felt that someone was watching her intently.

She didn't know what to make of Stephanie's story. She seemed sincere about it, but Sarah also reminded herself that she wasn't an expert at deciphering lies or even noticing when someone else was lying. She also knew that some women could be vindictive. She had been at times in her past. She had spread any lie she could think of to paint a person in a bad light—especially about the boyfriends who dumped her.

Sarah excused herself from the table. She had to get away from the tension in the air, yet she loathed going back into her cell. One side of the common room was designated as the exercise track. Forty feet of clear walking space. Sarah joined three other women making laps on the undersized oval. Walking in silence, she mulled the information through her head.

"Ugh," Sarah groaned to herself. "I don't understand it." She finished two more laps, then walked to her cell.

A male guard had just pulled her thin foam mattress off the top bunk. Another male guard was going through her personal belongings while a female officer stood at the entrance. Sarah wasn't worried that they would find anything. All she had in her personal file were photocopied papers of her temporary assignment to the jail for the court proceedings and a copy of her driver's license. She was just appalled at the indignity of the search.

"I thought my being present while you searched my belongings was proper protocol." Sarah was surprised at her authoritative voice. She assumed the known position of her hands behind her back and stood directly across the hall from her cell door. She stiffened her resolve to conform to a higher standard. Feet shoulders-width apart, she locked herself into parade rest.

"Random inspection, ma'am," the female guard said.

"I have a pen, an empty notepad, documentation that I am assigned here temporarily and a copy of my driver's license. This is the third random search that I have been subject to this week, out of the seven since I've been here. I'm curious to see if you find any imaginary contraband or if this is just professional supervised harassment."

"Sarah Menendez!" a voice called from the counsel room door.

"Please see that my lawyer gets an unedited video copy of each search. Please see that all four of my personal items get put back."

The three officers stared at her dumbfoundedly as she moved off to the counsel room. She grinned inwardly that she had one-upped them, even if it was for a mere moment; plus, she had a wealth of new information and questions for her attorney.

Chapter XXVI

Sarah seated herself in the same chair she used to sign herself into the hellhole that she was now viewing as heaven. It seemed a lifetime ago. That she was back here and facing one of her biggest demons was another reason she held her head high. She knew she was right. Whether or not anyone else believed her didn't seem to matter anymore.

She had topped the emotional hurdle of reliving a nightmare. Now everything she viewed in the county jail seemed to be more of a sideshow: inmates throwing around clout to try and be important, guards pulling petty power trips that were still within the confines of their assigned tasks. She had a growing appreciation for the by-the-book type of officers.

"Good afternoon, Miss Sarah." Mr. Henderson smiled at his charge, adopting the proper address that the academy used.

"Good afternoon, sir." Sarah scooted her chair in to the table, then rested her hands atop it.

"How has your day been?"

"It's been interesting."

"Oh really. How so?" Mr. Henderson set his briefcase on top of the table, preparing to open it.

"I learned that there are a few women in town that swear that Mike is the father of their kids. One was recently arrested on his property. She said she was trying to get some medical background from him, as her child is sick with something that the doctors can't figure out. She thinks that understanding some of his medical background might help diagnose what to do for her son."

"Mildly interesting, but not likely to help our case."

"And just now, before I came in here, they were searching my belongings without me present. Out of all the 'random' searches they did, my few items were searched three times out of the seven. I told them that you will want any unedited copies of the searches. Their faces looked like I had caught them with their hands in the cookie jar."

"Just now?"

"Yes, sir. I left to come in here and they were still searching my things."

"Excuse me. I'll be back in a few minutes," Mr. Henderson said and toted his briefcase out the door.

****

Sarah settled into a solitary cell in a neighboring county jail. If she was needed in court, it would be an hour shuttle in shackles. She was allowed a kiosk for an hour in the morning and an hour in the evening as it rotated through the solitary cells of the fluctuating inmate population. She used the nightly kiosk time to watch an hour's worth of TV and the morning kiosk time to call Dean Vickery for a daily check-in.

Her lawyer had put ten dollars on her account if she should have a need to call him. She was issued a few stamped envelopes and a half dozen pieces of paper.

She leaned over the small shelf and began scribbling out a letter to Dean Vickery. As she wrote her appreciation for the academy and all it had taught her, a TV talk show filled the small concrete cavern with distracting noise.

So, the initial test showed that you weren't the mother, the hostess said, reaffirming what her guest had said earlier.

Yes. We did a dozen paternity tests. They all showed my husband to be the father, but I wasn't the mother. And I thought, how could this be? I watched this child come out of me. How could this child not be mine? He did not leave my room. My husband was there the whole time as well.

I bet that was frustrating. Everyone knows the stereotype of a man saying they're not the father, but it is unheard of to hear of a mother not being the mom, the host said, playing up the drama that made for better ratings in an ever-competitive field of entertainment.

It was frustrating to no end.

So, what happened next? How did you solve the riddle?

We consulted a new doctor.

What did that doctor say?

He said he wanted to run a few tests and actually go in for a minor procedure to take a tissue sample from my ovaries and an egg to have tested.

Here today is the man who solved this couple's riddle as well as three dozen others.' He's an accomplished family practitioner and bestselling author for the book "Who is My Mommy?" You can follow him on social media and his website. Please welcome Dr. Phil Bluckman.

The crowd gave an enthusiastic applause for the handsome middle-aged doctor as he waved to the crowd and walked to an open seat next to the mother.

Tell us how you met and what you learned about this mom who isn't a mom to her beautiful son, said the hostess.

Sarah was now transfixed by the information streaming through the kiosk screen. She devoured every bite it was sending out. Before the program concluded, she was dialing her attorney's number.

Chapter XXVII

"You crashed the truck," Mackenzie said.

"Ugh. It's impossible. I don't see how anyone can back that truck into that dock. It's too narrow." Kimberly complained about the narrow alley and the ninety-degree jackknife docking the simulator set up for them.

Three large screens provided a wraparound view of the windows and the simulated environment. The air ride seat had been pulled out of a Peterbilt truck after the original was worn out from its previous installation. A standard transmission with multiple range selectors stood next to the seat. Digital gauges and an e-log computer were mounted facing the driver to give a real-world simulation.

"The program says that it's possible," Temperance said. She had tried and failed three times as well.

"Can we widen it out just a little bit?" Kimberly asked.

"No! Ya whiney little shit," Harris barked. "How long's the trailer?"

"Forty feet."

"What kind of tractor is it?"

"Short day cab. Like those brown ones you used to drive when I was little," Temperance said.

Harris stood and started swinging his cane in front of him, fumbling his way to the simulator. "What size are the tires?"

"Twenty-two five," Temperance answered.

"Does it show the lug nuts on your screen?"

"No."

"What about tire markings?"

"Yes. I can change the image to show a painted tire mark."

"Line the truck up so the driver's seat is at the beginning side of the dock."

Temperance reset the simulator.

"Now, pick a wheel mark and tap something on the table every time that wheel mark hits the ground."

"Yes, sir." Temperance addressed her father as if he were any other teacher.

"What do you pansy asses want to bet that I can do this. Fifty dollars?"

"We're not allowed to bet, sir," Teresa said.

"Fucking sissies," Harris grumbled. "I ain't gonna do it if there's nothing in it for me."

"If you lose, you have to wear a dress for the next week," Mackenzie piped up.

"I ain't wearing no goddamn dress."

"What if we can bet something that will improve us? Improve all of us?" Teresa asked.

"What do you mean?" Temperance finished entering the adjustments into the simulator.

"What if we say that Mr. Harris can order us around? We'd have to do anything he says," Teresa concluded.

A grin spread from ear to ear as Harris's mind flooded with possibilities.

Temperance saw the grin. It terrified her to imagine what was going through her father's mind. She bolted to her feet. "Nothing sexual! Nothing illegal! And *nothing* against the academy's rules."

Harris's grin dissolved into a frown. All the fun had just escaped his grasp. "And two of you have to give up your desserts every day. I prefer chocolate cake and apple pie. I'm actually really fond of pie."

Temperance had to stifle a gag—the perverted image he implied turned her stomach. "One dessert and two weeks," she barked at him.

Harris grumbled again.

"And if Mr. Harris wins, whatever he says has to be geared toward learning how to drive," Temperance added.

Harris grinned and settled into the simulator.

****

Sarah hummed a happy tune and prepared herself for the fast-paced learning challenge ahead. She was back amid familiar surroundings—a place she had dearly missed. She hadn't thought she would, but the women around her were becoming more like family than anyone else ever had. Adjusting her business textbooks to form a neat row across the top of her desk, she turned to leave for the cafeteria. After lunch she would be diving back into her studies. She felt this time that she would be more enthusiastic about the program, as a big chunk of the puzzle had just been found.

She had been told that the court case was postponed, pending a new DNA review. She only hoped that things would finally come to light and that the other women she had mentioned to her attorney would be able to find the answers they sought as well.

THE CLASSROOM

Sarah left her room and headed to the cafeteria.

"Click, click, click, click, click, click. Quarter turn right. Click, click, click. Half turn left. Brake. Half turn right. Reverse. Click, click—"

Sarah almost bumped into Temperance and Harris as Temperance escorted her father down the hall.

"What the heck did I miss?" Sarah asked, falling in step with Temperance as they headed to the cafeteria.

"We lost a bet," Temperance said. Harris chuckled as he held her arm, following behind the CDL class as they each drove their own imaginary trucks to the cafeteria.

They marched through the halls, clicking each time their left foot hit the ground and turning their imaginary steering wheels one way, then the other. After a prescribed number of clicks forward, they marched backward at a half step, clicking as their left foot struck the ground. Each foot stepped in rhythm with Teresa, the cadence caller, on the left. The smattering of students on the right marched in a single file line, arms stretched out in front as if holding steering wheels at arm's length.

"Mr. Harris says that public embarrassment is the best way to learn a lesson," Temperance continued.

"I'm gonna go talk to the dean after lunch," Harris interjected. "See if he'll put up a stockade. Then you can throw your rotten food at the disorderly students. They'll learn real fast."

"No. You dirty old man. That is not the reason you want a stockade. No. Bad Harris," Temperance said, and turned him into a corner.

His chuckle was cut off by the sudden jolt from connecting with the brick wall. "Damn, girl. You tryin' to kill your old man?"

"Oh, I'm sorry. I was trying to think of a witty comeback. I must not have been focusing on my driving. I'll try to concentrate better. It's just so hard to concentrate on directions when someone is being rude."

"Your mama had road rage too," Harris said.

Temperance angled him into a corner again while suppressing a smirk.

"Damn it, girl," Harris spat as he rubbed his forehead.

"Oh. I'm so sorry. I must have gotten a little frazzled when you said something about my mama. I must have lost my concentration again. Did you know, Miss Sarah, that pain is a good teaching tool also?"

Harris groaned and muttered under his breath, then fell silent.

Sarah gave half a smile and followed the procession into the cafeteria.

"Miss Sarah."

Sarah halted at the familiar voice. "Yes, Dean Vickery?"

"Your meeting with Governor Reynolds was pushed back another week. Three weeks from today."

"Yes, sir." Sarah stood at parade rest in front of him.

"Are you ready?" Dean Vickery asked.

"Honestly, sir. I think you know the answer to that. I want to be in front of him right now arguing her case. As far as making the best argument that I can, I don't think I'll ever be ready."

"Well, whatever happens, always give it all you got. If you give everything you have, you won't have any regrets holding you back."

"Sir. What if I go too far? What if I start babbling? What if I start begging? I know that it doesn't help, but when I feel this strongly about the outcome, how do I keep my emotions in check?"

"If you find yourself begging, stop, take a breath, don't apologize, continue with the best reason that you can think of to show that she will better serve the community on the outside."

"Yes, sir."

"Honesty and integrity are what the governor's office respects. Once you have made your case, stand ready to accept their decision."

"Yes, sir."

"No matter what it is."

"Yes, sir."

Chapter XXVIII

Sarah sat in the polished limestone marble hallway in a tucked-away corner of Missouri's state capitol. She had studied the artwork of Thomas Hart Benton more than a dozen times over and read the summarization of his life on a plaque three times. Her appointment had come and gone, yet they still told her to wait. Her stomach growled almost constantly. The half dozen trips to the water fountain curbed her hunger for only a few minutes. Her 10 a.m. appointment was a distant memory, as 4 p.m. was coming up fast.

She approached one of the paintings for the umpteenth time. Her escort, Lataisha, sat in the corner and turned page after page of her inner-city romance novel. Her job was to monitor Sarah but let her have full decision-making management of her expedition and only step in if the decisions made were outside of the itinerary.

Sarah didn't study the intricate brushstrokes; instead she closed her eyes and mentally went through all the things she wanted the governor to know about. She would tell him about Gloria's family, the work she did at the academy, the noble heart she had shown to save a broken-down jezebel. She would lay out letters from countless people in her hometown recounting times when Gloria had helped them and asked nothing in return.

She would then tell the governor of how Gloria came to be in the academy, but she would leave out the excuse of taking on her sister's blame, as it was not respectable to do such a thing.

Sarah had worked every available hour on learning everything she could about asking the governor for Gloria's pardon. She gathered letters and proofread them to make sure they were legible, grammatically correct and aligned with her overall goal.

Many phone calls were blocked and doors were slammed in her face when she tried to get support for Gloria's case. It was like hauling boulders to the top of the hill all over again. There was no reason, only that it had to be done. With every defeat came the search for another door to knock on.

Governor Reynolds had canceled his appointment just minutes after Sarah arrived at the state capitol. "What do you mean, he had an emergency?" Sarah was about to come apart. Her blood was boiling, and her mind was on the verge of shedding into a million pieces. She found that all the values that were taught at the academy didn't seem to translate to regular people; those values were not seared into their minds with the morality of respect.

One of the governor's assistants, whom Sarah had scored a meeting with after the governor's cancelation, suddenly had to leave. It was explained to her that it was a family emergency. She did her best to hide her frustration and her ankle monitor, but the ankle monitor became a glaring billboard of embarrassment whenever she sat down, causing many to detour away from her. Another assistant promised to see that she was taken care of, though she didn't say how. Her original ten o'clock meeting was changed to two-thirty, and it was now after four. She tried to remain calm, but her nerves were completely overwhelmed from the waiting. The twinge of panic she had been fighting off crept back into her brain.

"Excuse me, sir." Sarah approached the uniformed security guard. His dark blue uniform stretched against the black skin encasing the gym-honed bulk that could easily intimidate or wrestle under control anyone stepping out of line.

He turned to check her for any potential threat. He didn't speak, but softened his stance to invite her to continue. He had long ago eyed the ankle monitor and studied her clutching the file folder reverently. He assumed it was of great importance, at least to her anyway, as she had been holding it with both hands most of the time.

"When do you start ushering people out the door?"

"In about thirty minutes, ma'am."

"Thank you."

"Why are you here, if you don't mind my asking?"

Sarah hesitated at divulging any information, but reconsidered, as the moral reason might be considered favorably, swaying the governor to side with her. "I traded a wonderful crab dinner to Dean Vickery for a five-minute audience with Governor Reynolds."

"Dean Vickery? Which school are you from?" Officer Williams asked.

"The Schultz Business Academy."

"I've never heard of it."

"It's a boot camp for selected convicts who want to turn their life around and start doing good things for their community. We are asked to define two goals; one personal and one community based, to fulfill our souls and make the world a better place to live."

"So that explains your ankle monitor."

Sarah blushed a little from the shame of having to wear the monstrosity.

"What's your community goal?" Officer Williams asked, settling into a more relaxed mood now that the day was drawing to a close.

"I really don't have one. Not yet, anyway. I haven't thought that far into the future."

"What about your personal goal?"

"My personal goal is to get a pardon for the one person who believed in me enough to risk prison in order to save me from it."

"How'd she do that?"

"She broke the rules at the academy in order to show me that I was worth more than what most people thought and more than what I thought of myself."

Sarah clutched the folder to her breast, compressing the custom-tailored suit that she had helped make. She had split her time between working for the tailor, studying at the library and attending her business classes and the mandatory therapy sessions at the academy.

"I see. Well good luck to you. I've heard that the governor isn't very lenient on pardons."

Sarah's heart dropped. She nodded to him and turned back to the bench where she had fidgeted for the past several hours. Sitting down, she opened the folder with the first letter from a local grocer who knew Gloria to help customers even though she didn't work there. One such customer insisted that Gloria be given a raise and wouldn't leave until the manager agreed to it. Sarah reverently closed the folder and hiked up her pant leg at the pinch brought on by the ankle monitor.

The black hard plastic case with a metal frame, rubber-coated steel-mesh cable and keyed lock held fast to her ankle. It was heavier than the standard ones they had to wear in the academy. The larger battery and amped transmitter allowed the academy to see where she was, even in most buildings, unless she went into a basement or a subway where she couldn't be tracked on their computer.

Those who worked offsite at the restaurant wore them, as well as any student who had to make a trip outside of the school's perimeter.

It was a grueling process to be allowed to travel to the state capital to do this one thing. In addition to planning all the stops and alternate routes, any foreseeable emergency had to be taken into account with a plan to overcome or avoid it if there was a complication. She had the plan drilled into her head. All the stops they were to make, whether she needed them or not. Of the two stops on the way to Jefferson City, she only needed to use the restroom once. Her packed lunch was now gone, and she had only one bottle of water for the return trip. Now she was being delayed, which meant that she had to answer her assigned phone every fifteen minutes to state why she was being delayed.

"Excuse me, miss."

Sarah hurried to put her pant leg down at the sound of a woman's voice. She looked up to see a well-dressed woman who looked to be in her early fifties.

"Are you here to see someone?"

Sarah bolted to her feet and quickly straightened her suit. "Yes, ma'am. I was to have an audience with Governor Reynolds at ten this morning. I was told that unfortunately he had to cancel, but I was supposed to meet with an adviser who also had to cancel his appointment due to an emergency at home. Yet I was told again to wait because I might be able to see someone who would be able to listen to my case."

The woman stared with an unreadable face, considering the authenticity of her words. "Officer Williams."

200

"Yes, ma'am."

"How long has this young lady been waiting here?"

"I came on shift at noon. She has been here since at least that time."

The woman nodded, appraising Sarah's integrity. "Don't go anywhere, Mr. Williams." Her authoritative tone caught Sarah off guard. She straightened her slim form with a confidence Sarah assumed that she would never be able to attain herself. "Miss, what's your name?"

"Sarah Menendez, ma'am."

A spark of recognition ignited in her eye. "You're not here on behalf of your father, are you?"

Sarah almost vomited on the spot. The woman took half a step back at seeing the instant reflex.

"No, ma'am." Sarah composed herself. "I am here on behalf of someone whom I believe is insurmountable in the kindness of her heart and lives her life on the same level as the pope, Gandhi, and maybe even Jesus."

The beautifully sophisticated woman studied Sarah even more, due to the boastful depiction of the young woman's friend. She glanced down at the ankle monitor that was barely hidden when Sarah stood and became blazingly apparent when she was seated. She then glanced at her companion, recognizing the insignia of the academy on her shoulder patch.

Lataisha continued to sit on the bench, reading her novel. Her job was only to be the driver and backup communication in case Sarah decided not to follow the academy's rules or to attempt an escape.

"Wow. That is certainly a flattering compliment for your friend," the primped woman said. "I'm certain you're not talking about my husband. He's a good man, but being a politician, jumping the fence from one side to the other is a requirement for the job."

Sarah reciprocated the woman's pleasant smile. "I was to have an appointment with Governor Reynolds at ten this morning. It was canceled. Then I was to meet with a Mr. Gregory . . ."

"Gregory Gibbons," the woman finished for her. "He likes to throw his weight around, even though he is outranked by many in the capitol."

"I was told he left."

"Not likely. He is nosy and is always up in everybody's business. My suggestion is that you limit any information you give him. Why are you still here?"

"I was told to wait. That I still might be able to speak to somebody to plead for my friend's pardon."

"What organization are you with?"

"I'm from the Schultz Business Academy. It's a—"

The woman held up her hand to stop her. "I'm familiar with the academy. I've met Mr. Schultz on several occasions. He's a very smart man. Many people opposed his building the academy, but I'm glad he did. I've seen so many girls come out of there and do so many different and extraordinary things. One of those young ladies owns a delicatessen downtown. She makes a wonderful avocado salsa. I won't buy it anywhere else. I'm sorry, you must be on a schedule. Let's see about getting someone to see you."

A loud grumble emitted from Sarah's stomach.

The woman glanced at Sarah's middle. "Yes, and we'll take care of that too."

Sarah looked at the woman, unsure of what she was talking about.

"Mr. Williams," the woman addressed the security guard.

"Yes, ma'am."

She turned to Sarah. "Would a cup of fruit and some crackers spell you for a while?"

Sarah nodded, caught up in not offending anyone. Though food had been the furthest thing from her focus, hunger suddenly caught up to her and complained loudly.

"Mr. Williams, can you call the deli downstairs and have someone bring up a cup of fruit, crackers and a sweet tea for this young lady? Have them put it on my bill."

"Yes, ma'am." Officer Williams turned his hulking frame to the information desk and picked up the phone.

"Now." The woman turned back to Sarah. "Shall we go see what happened to your appointment?"

"Ma'am, I was told to wait here, and someone would come get me."

"Am I not someone?"

Sarah panicked. She wasn't sure if she should wait for the young man who said he would be back or go with this woman to somewhere she didn't know. "Yes ma'am, you are."

"Come along, sweetie; let's see if we can find the right person to talk to." The woman turned and started away.

When Sarah hesitated, the woman stopped and turned and found fear in her eyes. She saw the fear of the unknown and that of an untrusting soul.

"Miss Sarah."

Sarah looked into her kind and gentle eyes.

"I know you're in a strange environment, but we are all people. Had my circumstances been different growing up, I might be in your shoes. Scared out of my mind of the uncertainty, and if you had been brought up differently, do you think you might lend a hand to a frightened child and walk them back to the security of their parents?"

Sarah nodded. "Yes, ma'am. I believe I would."

"We're all just plain people doing our best to make this world a little better. If you come with me, I promise nothing bad will happen to you."

Sarah nodded again. "Yes, ma'am." Sarah glanced at Lataisha, who tucked her book into her bag, and the two followed their host down a corridor to a smaller, more intimate waiting room.

"Please wait here on the bench. I'll see if the governor will make time to see you," the woman said as she disappeared behind a pair of large mahogany doors.

Chapter XXIX

"D"amn, woman. Can't you drive?" Harris looked out of the corner of his eye and recognized the blazing red *FAIL* on the screen.

"I don't get it. What am I doing wrong? Why did I fail?" Kimberly asked.

"You ran over the line three times," said Temperance.

"It was only just a little bit."

"It still counts. You have to watch both mirrors."

"Aww, hogwash," Harris said. He would have used a stronger word except he didn't want to provoke another ill-timed shower from his daughter. "You only need one mirror. Your problem is not understanding when to start straightening out the tractor."

"Sir, how will I know when it's time to turn the wheel back?" Kimberly asked.

"These damn computer screens don't give you a sense of actually turning. You don't have the sun to help navigate, nor any other surroundings to judge when you're in the correct position." Harris fidgeted in his chair, then leaned on his cane.

"Sir, there's no way anyone can do this, surroundings or not. This is an accurate true-to-life simulator. It's just not possible."

"I've had thirty years of seeing what I was doing. After twenty years I could do it all blindfolded, and the last two years I faked good eyesight just to keep my job. Now I can't see a goddamn thing. I'm stuck here with a bunch of wannabe truck drivers. I can't teach you without a truck."

"Why not, sir?" Elisa leaned forward, ready to gain any knowledge that spilled out.

"Because it's a machine, it has a soul just like some of you. Some machines have an attitude all their own, just like a woman with PMS. You have to feel the machine and listen to its heartbeat. You have to understand what that machine is doing. Understand what it's telling you. That goddamn—"

"Harris!" Temperance barked at him, imploring him to watch his language.

"Oh, shut the hell up. Go get the damn hose if you want to." He turned back to the students. "That damn computer won't tell you a damn thing about driving on snow and ice."

"Why not, sir?"

"Because you won't be able to feel the rear end slip on icy roads. You won't feel the front wheel sink into a soft shoulder in the spring thaw and you won't feel the out-of-balance wheel from a blown tire or mud stuck in the rim. It won't send you the smell of antifreeze cooking off of your exhaust or the smell of the brakes burning because you forgot to release your Johnny bar.

"There's a thousand glorified steering wheel holders to just one trucker. If you turn on that damn radio, you ain't nothin' 'cept a glorified steering wheel holder. If you want to be a trucker, listen to that lump of bolts. It will tell all you need to know. Feel the gearshift. Listen to the engine. It will have its own rhythm.

"If you want to be a trucker, seek out a company that will assign you your own truck. When that truck is running smooth, you're making money and so is the company. If you get a job where you have to share a truck, you're not a trucker. You're just a butt in the seat to make the company money."

A knock reverberated from the door. Temperance got up and opened the door to the bright light outside. "Yes. Can I help you, Miss Fay?"

A construction student with a carpenter's pencil snugly held in a pocket on her left upper arm held a wooden contraption out to Temperance. "Miss Temperance, Mr. Harris ordered this for us to build and bring over to you."

"What is it?"

"It's a gearshift, you numbskull," Harris said, leaning on his white cane.

"Our simulator already has a gearshift." Temperance accepted the wooden box and set it down next to her father. "Thank you, Miss Fay," Temperance said, to be as respectful as possible of the hard work others had put into the contraption.

"You don't have one like this," Harris said.

"Why do we need one like this?" asked Temperance.

"Because this is how you're going to land your first job."

"What are you talking about, Mr. Harris?" Temperance was still uncomfortable calling him her father, let alone admitting that he was.

"Alright, you wannabes. Scoot closer and watch." Harris adjusted the box to his right and turned it until he was satisfied with its position. "If you're going to fit into a man's world, you're going to have to know as much or more than the boss or foreman does. Some of these outfits will want to put you to the test and see if you know your shit."

"Harris," Temperance growled at him.

"Oh for god's sake, spray me and be done with it, woman. I'm teaching a lesson here." Harris paused to see if any water would suddenly rain down on his head due to the cussing infraction. When nothing happened, he continued. "This is a six-by-four transmission. You can bet that some of these outfits still have a truck with these old transmissions in them. Sometimes it will be a five-by-four and sometimes they will make you drive one with three different gearshifts. We'll get to that one later.

"For now, I'll show you the six-by-four." Harris dove into his lecture as Temperance scooted forward, forgetting about the water hose.

****

"No. I won't accept it." Jamika glared at Dean Vickery.

"Jamika, it is this or prison." Dean Vickery spat back at a face full of defiance.

"No. I tolerated this only to get to my grandmother sooner. I am not going to do another round of this . . . BS." Jamika caught herself and corrected to something less vulgar.

Dean Vickery looked at the stubbornness that was entrenched in the woman's face. There was no other option. She was the best person for the job. He tried to convince her of that, but she would have none of it.

"Miss Jamika, I've called all of our outreaches and they all have full plates and refuse to deal with your antics. Now, if you want my blessing on your marriage to Landon, you had best consider this." Dean Vickery threw out a bluff. Most of the counselors at the outreach did have full plates managing the students who were reentering society. He knew a few would have taken her on, but they were in an area that was too close to her old environment.

One place wasn't, but it was in rural Montana, and he was sure Jamika would have a bigger fit about that than what she was throwing now. "Look Miss Jamika, you are the only one I know that I can count on to do this." He pulled out three different contracts and slid them to her. "I know that there's only one thing you like about this area and I know he can put in a transfer to follow you wherever you go. Sorry, I was bluffing a bit. There is one opening in rural Montana. It is a small town, but I have a feeling you won't like it. So, here are the three contracts. Finish your prison sentence. It's only nine more months or one of the other two. Each has a two-year contract. I really hope you choose the one I mentioned.

"I don't want to pressure you, but a decision has to be made today. Regardless of which one you choose, you leave tomorrow."

"What about Landon?"

"Best I can offer is, write him a letter. I'll leave you to your decision." Dean Vickery walked out of the counselor's office and back to his own.

Chapter XXX

Sarah stood in front of Governor Reynolds's desk as he conversed with a young man wearing a dark gray suit. From the low and hurried tones, she guessed that they were almost finished with their conversation, which sounded more like instructions from the governor to what she guessed was an errand boy. She held the file folder tight to her chest and tried not to fidget by biting the inside of her lip to stave off the rising panic that urged her to run back out the door.

White oak bookshelves lined one wall. Most looked like lawbooks, except in the far corner by the office's window—a small collection of coloring books sat neatly arranged with a box of crayons. The man's desk was the size of a pool table with nothing sitting atop it except for his elbow. Opposite the bookshelves was a computer desk with a cabinet hutch above. The desk matched the white oak bookshelves but contrasted the black frames and dark screens of the dual monitors.

Next to the computer was a stack of corner shelves. Various antiques that looked like they came from sunken ships sat singly or two to each shelf, with ample room for more objects. One looked like a rusted cannonball, another a cracked ceramic jug. Sarah assumed that it had held rum at one time. The other objects were not as distinguishable, and she couldn't make out what they might have been used for.

An older gentleman sat in an overstuffed leather chair next to the antique seafaring tools. His completely white hair was still very thick, and it piled high atop his head. If he had had a beard, Sarah was sure that she would be able to see him every December at the mall listening to every child talk about their wish list. If she still believed in those miracles, she would wish her friend out of prison. The Santa Claus she wanted to speak to was still talking in a hushed tone to the young man in the gray suit.

She caught the white-haired gentleman glancing her way, seeming to be mildly curious to how she presented herself. He kept checking on her, though he pretended to be fully engaged in the conversation that Governor Reynolds was locked into. Sarah stood clutching her folder tightly as if someone might jump, snatch it from her and toss it out the window. The slightest of a smirk turned up the corner of his mouth. The older man wore a black sport coat, white button-down shirt and black pants, but he was missing a tie. She thought that it would be odd for any man to be missing a tie when addressing the governor.

Sarah thought the lack of a tie would show him as less of a person, but it didn't for this man. The way he carried himself, sated in the chair and directing his attention one way then the other at his own command, perplexed her. It was as if he was far superior to the governor himself, yet he treated the governor with respect and didn't seem the slightest bit annoyed by the extended conversation the governor was having with the young man.

Sarah thought she was going to feel creeped out, but the man had a perpetual glint in his eye—he seemed genuinely delighted that she was there. She thought he looked like the wise grandfather checking to see if she was behaving herself. He interjected a time or two, correcting a couple pieces of data and emphasizing a section from the spreadsheet. To Sarah, it sounded like a construction project. The terms *ground work, fencing* and *building supplies* all meant more work for Missouri's vibrant economy and the challenges to keep the construction cost to a manageable level.

"Yes sir, I'll get those details to you first thing next week," the young man said. He closed his folder and turned to leave. "Miss." He nodded at Sarah, then walked around her and out the door.

Sarah's eyes followed him out the door, then turned back to Governor Reynolds. His penetrating gaze sliced right through her opening line. She opened her mouth to speak, but nothing came out. A long second ticked by. Her panic escalated exponentially. Her instincts told her to bolt out the door, following the young man who had just left, but she stood there slack-jawed like a boy who just saw his first set of breasts.

"I hear you traded a delicious crab dinner for a five-minute audience with me." Governor Reynolds leaned back in his chair. "I think you better make that crab dinner count."

Sarah pulled her mind back to the present. He was right. She had to make every second count. She cleared her throat and began.

"Honorable Clarence Reynolds, thank you for finding time in your busy schedule to listen to my plea.

"My name is Sarah Menendez. I'm a student at the Schultz Business Academy. As per the academy's requirements, we are asked to create one goal to help the community and one individual goal that we want to attain for ourselves. My personal goal is to ask that a pardon be given to Miss Gloria Witcom. I have amassed a collection of letters

212

from her family, friends, neighbors, work associates, and fellow drills from the Schultz Business Academy.

"Miss Gloria has exemplary recommendations from all of her colleagues and bosses. Each one has stated in their letters that they would hire her back at a moment's notice. She was involved in her church before her admittance to the academy and organized a small prayer group and bible study Sunday afternoons in her hometown. I have a letter from Dean Harold Vickery stating his opinion on the prospects of her future outside of incarceration."

"May I see the letter from Dean Vickery?" Governor Reynolds asked.

"Yes, sir." Sarah set the thick folder down on the edge of his desk and pulled his letter off the top, as she figured that this was one that he might want to read. Handing it to the governor, she stepped back and waited.

"Have you read all the letters?" the governor asked.

"Yes, Your Honor."

"Are they all peaches and cream?"

"All but two, Your Honor."

"Two? Tell me about the two?"

Setting the folder back down on his desk, Sarah pulled one off the bottom of the pile. She took a step back and began.

"*Honorable Governor Reynolds,*

"*I have known Gloria Witcom for several years. She is a shrewd, scheming person. She is vivaciously vindictive. She has undermined the reputation of myself and others who are close to me. She is merciless in her attack of our reputation.*

"*If you grant her a pardon, you can expect that during the next election, my bowling team and I will not be voting for you. If she is allowed to come home, our winning streak will surely be over.*

"*Otherwise, she's a cool cat and a good mom.*

"*Sincerely, Ragina Evans, Occupation: Clerk of District Courts.*"

Governor Reynolds stopped tapping his pen atop his knee. He looked at Sarah over the top of Dean Vickery's letter. "That's what it says?"

"Yes, sir."

"What about the other one?"

Sarah fished out the other letter from the bottom of the stack.

"*Governor Reynolds,*

"*I sincerely ask that Gloria Witcom not be given a pardon. Our bowling team has had amazing success since she has been absent from the league. Her taunts in the bowling alley have made me consider counseling. My son is finally winning cross-country races since Gloria's son has dropped out to help his grandmother manage the house and his younger brothers.*

"*Fortunately, her bullying doesn't extend beyond the bowling league. I hear that she is pleasant to be around though I've never had the opportunity.*

"*Sincerely, Kim Armstrong. Occupation: domestic engineer.*" Sarah concluded reading the letter.

"And what of your experience with Gloria Witcom?" Governor Reynolds asked.

Sarah was afraid of this question. She knew it was going to be asked and had practiced her answer numerous times, but each time, she broke down when she realized her role in sending her away. It was maddening to break down in front of a mirror—it would be mortifying to break down in front of the governor.

She straightened her stance, took a deep breath and began.

"Honorable Governor Reynolds, I was on a destructive path that had a good chance of putting me in an early grave. There is no telling what I might have done or who I might have hurt. Gloria Witcom saved me from that fate. For right here and right now, I owe her everything within me to do the best I can under her principles as well as the values she taught me at the academy. I also owe the founders of the system that I am in. That system eventually brought our paths together. Without those individuals who care enough to better our community, I wouldn't have the opportunity that I have now to see life and its amazing potential.

"In the Schultz Business Academy, where I have been studying, I was not just taught but ingrained with seven core values, as was Miss Gloria. Two of those values she demonstrated have allowed me to see the strength and persistence it took to save me. They are 'duty' and 'selfless service.'

"She knew there was something buried deep inside me and she wouldn't let up until she uncovered it. By breaking the rules of the academy, she forced me to reveal what was holding me back.

"Your Honor, it was her duty to do everything she could to see that I had the best chance possible to succeed in life, and it was her selfless service that gave her the permission to break the rules for the benefit of the outcome.

"I cannot think of any circumstance where someone would be more deserving of being allowed to continue living their life and raising their family. I pray that you can find that everything here in this folder and what I have said is true and believable and that you would grant Miss Gloria Witcom a pardon."

Sarah exhaled and relaxed, as she had delivered the best heartfelt speech she thought she could muster. But a split second after she thought that she could relax and stave off a panic attack, a new and more troubling anxiety surfaced. She wondered if he would deny the pardon request. Her chest clenched tighter with every nanosecond that Governor Reynolds didn't respond.

He sat in the high-backed leather chair, looking at her with an unreadable face. The seconds threatened to turn into a full minute before he flinched a muscle. Leaning forward, he set the letter he was holding on his desk and looked at her again—drawing out a full minute as she stood in silence.

"It is out of the norm to listen to a presentation from someone about pardoning an individual . . . especially if that someone is currently incarcerated. However, I believe you made a very compelling argument. I'll have all the facts looked into, and make my decision at a later time. I commend you on your efforts. I know that it takes a great deal of courage to stand in front of a crowd, or anyone whom you want to ask a large favor of, and especially from a mayor, a governor or a president."

Governor Reynolds stood in preparation to see her to the door, then he stopped. He looked at her quizzically. "Are you the Menendez that's been on the news lately?"

Sarah was caught off guard. She wasn't prepared to answer this question. She didn't know how to answer. She thought about acknowledging that she was. Maybe it would gain her a couple of favoritism points. She couldn't deny it, as embarrassing as it was. But that would invalidate her visit and make any chance of getting Gloria a pardon nonexistent. She wouldn't allow that. The question demanded an answer, but which one should she give? She couldn't let this opportunity slip away. She couldn't ignore the question. She had to say something.

"Sir, I'm sorry that I'm unable to answer that question, both in a legal sense and it would be disrespectful if I were to put Miss Gloria's request below anything else at this time."

"Phillip, what do you think?" Governor Reynolds turned toward the grandfatherly gentleman sitting quietly in the chair.

"Miss Sarah, I apologize for the lack of a formal introduction earlier. My name is Phillip Schultz."

After several seconds of processing, Sarah's brain made the connection. Her eyes turned up to the tall, lanky man with a hint of a potbelly. "Sir. Oh. Sir." Sarah's excitement grew to that of god-worthy praise. "Thank you for setting up the academy. Myself and all the women there are so grateful for a chance to really turn our lives around. After seeing a few friends' failed attempts in local programs, I'm so grateful for the opportunity to learn where I was in life and the future of my path.

"I've never seen so many people who are trying so hard to better their lives, and the program makes it so much easier to see the rewards of all the good things that are available to us.

"We do have our moments when we get a bit . . ." Sarah paused, searching for the right word. "Frustrated," she said after failing to find one that seemed stronger than *frustrated*. "But the counselors are top notch and know when and how to ask us the right questions to help us solve our own problems."

"Good. I'm glad that everything is going so well." Phillip produced a broad grin, happy to hear such wonderful news directly from a student. "How are you doing on your studies?"

"I'm keeping pace with most of my peers, except recently, due to—" Sarah stopped before she divulged more than she was supposed to. She feared that they already knew who her father was because of the extensive media coverage about the high-profile case.

Phillip saw that she balked at divulging any more information about her father and the court case her father was vigorously contesting. Phillip had already pieced the information together and saw no cause to pry for any details. "That's good, Miss Sarah," Phillip said, seeing the apprehension on Sarah's face. "I have no doubt that you'll get caught back up."

"Thank you, sir."

"How did you get here?" Governor Reynolds asked.

"Miss Lataisha accompanied me here today," Sarah said, indicating the stocky woman standing just inside the door.

Phillip turned his attention to the woman. "Thank you, Miss Lataisha, for seeing both of you safely to Jefferson City."

"No problem, sir. Miss Sarah is a grand traveling companion."

"Will you be heading back tonight?"

"Yes, sir. As soon as we're done here."

Phillip turned to look at Governor Reynolds. "Clarence, do we need anything more from these ladies?"

"No. I think we should let them get back on the road. I believe they still have a few hours' drive ahead of them.

"Miss Sarah, Miss Lataisha, thank you for stopping by." Governor Reynolds moved around the desk and shook hands with Sarah, then Lataisha. "Good luck on your studies, Miss Sarah. Drive safe, Miss Lataisha."

Sarah thanked the governor and walked out into the hallway. Lataisha followed. A scream raked the air like nails across a chalkboard.

Chapter XXXI

Sarah and Lataisha froze just a few steps down the corridor outside the governor's office. Governor Reynolds and Phillip Schultz emerged behind them, staring down the empty hall.

"What the . . . ," a voice whispered behind Sarah as they strained to hear any more clues to the mysterious bloodcurdling scream.

A blur of movement flashed across the hallway. A woman wore a tattered and torn green sweater, faded jeans and dirty, worn-out shoes. Her ratted mess of hair and dirty tear-stained face gave the impression of a wild woman who had escaped the insane asylum. Her eyes, wide with wild determination, sought an escape from her pursuer.

A hulking blue uniform spun around the corner, just feet behind the crazed woman. Mr. Williams, a former Crimson Tide linebacker with many years of training from high school, college and the police force, bore down on his target as if he were still wearing shoulder pads and a helmet. The gritted teeth and fierce determination on his face likened him to a wolf ready to snatch his prey.

Governor Reynolds took a step forward, ready to block the possible assailant from getting to Sarah. He began to bend down, ready to take the blow, when a meaty fist grabbed the woman by the back of the pants, hauling her to a stop, then hoisting her into the air. Her arms and legs flayed as she whipped about, trying to break free, but the iron grip on her pants was immediately doubled as Williams's other arm encircled her waist.

Wild and crazy eyes peered out from the mess of hair that flailed erratically from the vicious tug-of-war between the woman and the hulking security guard. A pause from the woman allowed Williams to pin her to the floor and pull out his handcuffs. The wild eyes stared at Sarah's ankle monitor, then turned up to her face.

"It was you!" the woman screamed. The high-pitched shrill seemed like it could break glass.

Sarah backed up a step, unsure of what might happen next. She had been conditioned to immediately back away from any fight unless there wasn't any place to back away to. For the purposes of acting the proper citizen, she and the other students cowed at any confrontation because someone serving a term in the state corrections department was less believable than someone who had never had a ticket. Though they were taught self-defense, it was drilled into their minds to use it only as a last resort.

"You sent my sister away to prison. You bitch. I won't ever get to see her again." The woman wiggled a hand out of Williams's grasp and waved it wildly. Williams tried grabbing her flailing arm, but not before she ripped an object out from under her shirt and flipped it toward the governor.

Lataisha dove in front of Governor Reynolds, almost knocking him back against the wall. She batted the object to the floor before crashing to the floor herself. She spun up to a knee, crouched and ready to face any other advance and keep anyone else from getting close to the woman in case she could produce another object and hurl it with the intent of inflicting harm.

The woman's screams were stifled as Williams pressed his massive hand onto her back, restricting her movements and carefully allowing her to breathe but making screaming a laboring ordeal. This took most of the fight out of her as he worked to pull her hands behind her back. Sarah had seen that her face was flush when she rounded the corner, like she had already exerted much of her energy to get there. Now, already out of breath, her lungs were crushed and unable to replenish her depleted oxygen.

Grabbing her outstretched arm, Officer Williams wrenched it back and snapped it into his handcuffs. He hauled the scroungy, unkempt woman to her feet. The woman didn't even catch half a breath before the verbal assaults lashed out at Sarah.

"You're going to burn in hell for what you did. You don't deserve my sister. I do. She's mine. Why are you trying to steal her away from me? You BITCH! You—"

A screech of pain shot from her mouth as Mr. Williams twisted her arm and started hauling her away. The wild hair, grimy skin and pungent odor reported that hygiene was not one of her priorities. Her worn-out shoes skidded across the polished floor as she tried in vain to stay and unleash more verbal assaults against Sarah.

Sarah sank back a step further, feeling more guilt piled on top of the mountain that was already on her shoulders. The bizarre moment passed, and the screams and assaulting words faded to silence as the woman was dragged into a room that security used as their base of operations. There she would be held until the police arrived.

Phillip stepped forward and helped Lataisha to her feet, then stood back to stare down the hall where the woman had disappeared.

Governor Reynolds whispered to the well-dressed woman who had escorted Sarah to the governor's office. Sarah had wondered about her quiet authority until she saw a picture of her and the governor in an intimate embrace. The woman was his wife. She disappeared into the office and came out with his phone and a couple pencils.

Phillip looked at the governor and motioned to the paper on the floor. "What was that? The thing that she threw at you."

"It looks like just a folded piece of paper." The governor stepped forward and knelt down. He accepted his phone and pencils from his wife, then proceeded to take pictures of the possible evidence. After snapping a couple pictures, he handed the phone to his wife. "Start a video. I'm going to unfold it and see what it is."

Using the eraser ends of the two pencils, Governor Reynolds unfolded the paper and stretched it out across the floor. He read it silently at first, then out loud for the rest to hear.

"Dear Governor,

"I am three days better, but I am still sick. Many people in town say that I should write you a letter. I went to a confession booth today. I need to talk to someone who would not judge me. I know many people do. I am not religious, but I needed guidance on what was eating at me. I am not well, but I am well enough to tell you that the drugs in the car were not my sister's. She is too good of a person to do that. The drugs were mine. It is my fault that I forgot them in the car.

"The pastor said I would be forgiven if I told the truth. I hope I have the courage to get this to you."

"There's a bunch of markings here that I can't make out. Then it says: *I am sick again. You must let her go. I didn't . . . I made her a bad person. Please . . .*

"*Gloria good. She my best sister. She needs her boys. I am lost. Please, she must find me.*

"She signed it Maddy Witcom," Governor Reynolds concluded.

Chapter XXXII

Sarah breathed a sigh of relief when she stepped back into her room and its comfortable surroundings. Gathering her nightclothes, she sat on the edge of the bed to take off her dress shoes and rub her ankle where the heavy ankle monitor had nearly rubbed the skin off.

The larger monitor gave off a stronger signal and was used by those going outside the academy's boundaries and operated off any cell phone tower in the area. For those who didn't need to go off the property, a lighter, more comfortable tracker was used with the interior monitoring system. From the "God's room," as some students joked, administration could pull students up on the campus map and see which corner of the room they were standing in and which way they were facing. It was a little disconcerting, but Sarah overlooked it as a temporary, necessary evil.

Slipping into her shower shoes, she trudged toward the changing room. The long day of traveling to the capital and back had exhausted her. Since her meeting was delayed so long, she and the guard escorting her had missed their scheduled dinner at an approved restaurant. The restaurant quickly became packed and it would have been a long wait for a table. After a phone call, they were approved to get some fast food, which they ate quickly and got back on the road.

Sarah had been ignoring a bit of a side ache during the last part of the trip home. Now it came on with force. She dropped her things outside the changing area and hurried to the toilets.

"Are you OK?" a voice called from the other side of the door.

"Is that you, Miss Helen?"

"Yeah."

"I think it was something I ate."

"Don't you know that after eating healthy for so long, your body rejects those golden meals?"

****

"Hey, Miss Sarah. How's it going? Did you get to see the governor?"

"Good morning, Miss Temperance. I did. Where have you been?"

"Oh geez. They sent me over to the men's prison. There were a dozen men whose licenses had expired and they were fixing to be released. They had the experience but just needed to brush up on their knowledge, a few new laws that are in effect and a quick skills refresher. Dean Vickery and Warden Jeffreys thought it would be a good test run of the program."

"How'd they do?"

"The very moment I walked into the class, one student whistled at me. He was taken straight to the hole. I later heard he would have a sixty-day stay."

"Ouch. Harsh," Sarah commented. "What happened after that?"

"The assistant warden stepped in, ripped everyone up one side and down the other. He said that if they didn't want to be professional then he would see that they all spent ninety days in the hole. After that, everything went off without a hitch. They all thanked me for conducting an informative class, familiarizing them with the latest electronic logs and the brushup on their skills.

"Overall, the rest were a great bunch of guys."

"Ooh. Look at the traveling teach. Out there makin' sure the roads are safe to drive."

Temperance smiled at the innocent tease. "Seeing that open road . . . I just wish I was out there right now."

"Are you back to teaching here now?" Sarah asked.

"Yup."

"How are you and your father getting along?"

"Harris and I?" Temperance corrected. She didn't want to recognize him as her father. His absence in her life had cut a deep scar that she kept picking at in her mind, keeping the wound fresh. "We're doing good. He's teaching us some things that we would never learn in the book or the simulator."

"Like what?"

"He had the construction students build a replica of a six-plus-four transmission shifter and had each of us memorize the pattern."

"What's a six-plus-four transmission?"

"It's basically two transmissions stacked together."

"Oh."

"He said that it's guaranteed that one of us will go to a job interview where they'll pull out some ancient dinosaur to use as the test drive vehicle. He said that we are entering what is traditionally a man's world and that if we want to be part of it then we need to know as much or more than they do."

"That makes sense, I think," Sarah said, not quite sure if she understood.

"Well, try and think of it like this. Because we have been in trouble in the past, we have to work extra hard to prove—"

"Miss Sarah?" a voice interrupted.

Sarah and Temperance turned to find Gearda approaching them.

"Miss Sarah, could I visit with you a moment?"

"Yes, Miss Gearda."

"See, Miss Temperance, when you're good at something, you're always in demand."

Sarah took her leave from Temperance and followed Gearda back toward her office and the dreaded counseling room. To Sarah it was like a torture chamber in some ways. Ever-prying questions focused on extracting any viable information from her so the counselors could use those puzzle pieces to create their own neatly arranged work of art to hang on a wall as a personal trophy.

She mentally reprimanded herself, as this woman had helped her solve one of the problems that had plagued her. Thus, it wasn't fair to group all therapists into the overly paid rent-a-friend category. At the moment, Sarah didn't have a significant friend who could help iron out all the problems in her life. In their silent walk to the therapist's office, Sarah rejected the idea that this was a prison. If it were not, would she still seek the advice that Gearda had? Would she still attend class even though it wasn't a requirement?

"Back there, you said 'When you're good at something, you're always in demand.' What did you mean by that?" Gearda asked.

"Oh. That," Sarah said, bringing her mind back to the present. "I guess I meant that I am trouble, therefore always in demand of your attention."

"Well you're not in trouble this time."

"Then I must be trouble for someone else," Sarah said cheerfully, then added, "I just hope it's not for you or anyone here at the academy."

Gearda was silent for several paces, waiting to turn the corner into a quieter hallway. Sarah felt the seriousness of what lay ahead. Worry came over her as the silence lingered. She wondered if she had properly signed out and back in the key to the law library. She had recently been awarded the job and responsibility to open the doors and watch over the lawbooks and reference books, helping other students to find the materials they were looking for. This also allowed her a bit of quiet time to study her own classes.

She wondered if she had offended someone at the capitol. To be disrespectful to anyone there would be a disaster, because she was a product and representative of the school. She didn't want to be the cause of any ill view of the school. The academy, in essence, acted as the parental influence that she wished she could have had. For Sarah, it seemed like an almost perfect balance of parental upbringing. But one thing she truly craved was the personal touch. It was achingly painful to refrain from any sort of affection.

The only contact allowed was a firm handshake to solidify a deal or a hand on a shoulder at arm's length as a symbol of camaraderie. Neither was affectionate and far from filling the crater with the one thing that she craved. Other classmates had their visitation on Sundays, limited to either the morning or afternoon sessions. Special visits on days other than Sunday had to be approved by the dean, as he wanted to keep the students' progress moving forward with minimal distractions.

Sarah craved someone to come and visit her, but she knew it was hopeless; there wasn't anyone whom the academy would approve. All of her former friends did their best to avoid law enforcement or anyone with a hint of authority unless they knew them to be corrupt. She was almost a year into the second part of the program and hadn't received one letter from friends or family.

She was told that one had arrived, but it was from an old acquaintance who was clearly a few cards short of a full deck. In the letter, he asked her not to reveal where his stash of drugs was and that the chickens wouldn't be harmed because he had put his drugs in two ziplock bags and a coffee can.

When questioned about the friend, Sarah admitted that she knew him, but didn't feel he was that close of a friend. She told the investigator that she felt that he had an infatuation with her but kept a distance due to her other overbearing friends.

"What's this about?" Sarah asked.

Gearda opened her office door. "Please have a seat."

Sarah took in Dean Vickery and her attorney. "Good afternoon sir, Mr. Henderson." Sarah greeted them warmly.

"Good to see you in good spirits, Miss Sarah. How are your classes going?"

"Horrible, sir."

"Oh. Why is that?"

"Well, you asked me to come here; therefore I'm not in class. So, at the moment, they're not going anywhere and that is bad. I'm thinking that I must be your favorite student since you keep calling on me and keeping me from my studies, making me finish later than I would normally finish. So, I'm assuming that's your tactical way of keeping me here longer—hence further confirmation that I'm your favorite student."

Mr. Henderson tried to stifle a laugh but failed. Through a barely suppressed laugh, he asked, "Miss Sarah, do you want a job?"

"Mr. Henderson, as great as that sounds, I don't believe you're serious about the offer. At the moment, my time is filled with catching up on my studies."

The dean grinned at the small retaliation against the attorney.

Mr. Henderson looked a bit sheepish at the comment. He straightened his posture and presented himself with more of a business attitude.

"Miss Sarah, we got the results back from the lab."

"They found that he is my biological father and the biological father of my daughter," Sarah said in a factual tone. "Now he's backpedaling and wanting to take a plea deal? Now you want my input to argue that it be kept in front of a jury."

Sarah stood gracefully and purposefully, since everyone else was standing. She held her head high and her shoulders back. Clasping her hands in front of her, she took in a breath and exhaled it slowly.

"In the short time that I've been here, I have learned many wonderful lessons. If I had had a half-decent childhood, I would have learned enough to keep myself out of trouble. To me, I didn't receive a scholarship. I received something much more valuable. Every one of the drills screamed at me to fail. I didn't understand until afterward that they were screaming for me to succeed.

"Unfortunately for me, I was too stubborn to open my eyes to what they were trying to teach me. It took a well-deserved paddling for me to wake up and see what was being taught.

"I had been self-centered and arrogant for a long time. I never understood the interconnected relationship of the community that surrounded me. How one act can cause a whole community to either chastise you or support you. It all depends on an individual's actions or the words that they use.

"After watching a documentary on chimeras, I knew how to tell you what to look for, Mr. Henderson. I knew that he was my father and of course I knew he was the father of my child. What I was missing was that one thing that would explain to everyone else what I knew for years. I just didn't know how to bring it to everyone's attention.

"After I made that phone call to you, there wasn't anything else that I felt I needed to do there. I could finally move on and continue my education.

"The world is my classroom, and I want to learn everything that I can, then help whomever I can."

Chapter XXXIII

The clink of metal on metal chimed into the rhythm of the bumps in the road. The dark windows did more than shade the sun from the interior; they were also warped to distort any view of the outside world. Trees became globs of green. The view forward was obstructed by a steel wall with a small window. From Gloria's perspective, only the white line on the road was visible. It hypnotized her mind into forgetting much of the trip, making the time pass faster but in a pathetically boring way.

She had become disoriented and unable to figure out the general direction that she was traveling. It was like driving all night to a new town and expecting the sun to rise on the right but seeing it come up on the left. She hated that feeling—the feeling of not being in control of her own bearings, and it frustrated her to no end.

Gloria stared at the shackles that bound her to the transport van. She was the last one in the van. Several other women had already been dropped off at a neighboring county jail. She was among those who were transferred to other counties in the continuous merry-go-round to save a few dollars from being directly housed in the penitentiary for their full term. However, at the last stop she was told that she had to reboard for the last leg of the trip.

She was directed to sit in the center seat. One of the guards asked what kind of music she liked, to which she replied that it didn't matter, as it had been years since she had had the chance to listen. A country music station was dialed in and she let the beat take her off to a semislumber.

Downshifts and several turns brought the transport to a halt. The engine cut off and she waited the several minutes that it took the guards to log their change of activity. One thing that they could do, that she couldn't after the long drive, was stretch. Oh, she wanted to stretch so badly, but the chain around her middle prevented her from doing more than stretch her legs.

Keys rattled outside the door of the van. A click of the handle, and the door was hauled open. The officer leaned his big frame through the door, unlocked the bolt that tethered her feet to the floor and unfastened the seatbelt. Setting a step stool on the ground outside the van, the guard gave her permission to exit the vehicle.

Bright light screamed into the open door as Gloria scooted to the edge of the seat, looking for the step stool. She hoped to soak up a few minutes of sunshine before embarking on what she was sure would be a long, dreary cell-pacing stay.

"Well, you've looked better," came a familiar voice.

Gloria squinted against the sun, seeking the face that she hoped would be attached to the voice that sent her anxiety through the roof. The tall, broad-shouldered man stepped out of the shadow of the building. The blank brick wall hid any identifying marks that would clue her in to what was going on.

"Dean Vickery? What are you doing here?"

"Well, I wanted to check up on my star pupil. That's okay, isn't it?"

"Yes, sir. Of course it is. But what's going on?"

"Officer Gilpatrick, Officer Warren, thank you kindly for transporting Miss Gloria here."

"If you would sign here, Mr. Vickery." Officer Gilpatrick held a clipboard out for Dean Vickery, just like any delivery driver would do.

Dean Vickery scribbled a signature on it and handed it back. He turned to Gloria. "You're not gonna run off and try to escape, are you?"

"No, sir. I'm not going to do anything that would extend my time."

"Good. I don't think we need those shackles anymore."

"Sir?"

"Warden Wallace is a good friend of mine. We had a long conversation about what to do with you."

The shackles came off and the two officers stowed their gear and left.

"Walk with me, would you?"

"Yes, sir."

Gloria accompanied Dean Vickery around the end of the building. Her breath caught. Green grass stretched across the vast field before it butted up against dense shrubbery and trees. The mountain loomed high over their heads. The various obstacle course structures disrupted the field at uneven intervals.

Even though it wasn't home, she still felt a familiar warmth from the surroundings. It had been hard work to prove her worth. As she did, she learned much more about herself and how she would conduct her life in the future. Dean Vickery led her to a pair of chairs set up behind the barracks: his plush office chair and a hard plastic stool.

Gloria went to sit down on the stool but was interrupted.

"No. No, that one's mine—for today anyway," Dean Vickery said.

Gloria looked around for another stool but there wasn't one in sight.

"Today you get my chair."

"Sir?"

"The terms of your incarceration have changed."

"I don't understand, sir."

"Oh, quit calling me sir. My name's Harold."

"Yes, sir." Gloria watched the man roll his eyes like a father would do when frustrated at dealing with a teenage daughter. "What kind of change are you talking about with my incarceration?"

Dean Vickery reached into a cooler and pulled out an ice-cold beer. He held it out to Gloria.

"Sir. I don't understand." She clutched one hand to the other, refusing to accept the beverage.

"You, Miss Witcom, are free to leave."

"What?"

"You are free to get up and walk the hell out of here."

"You're joking, right? Is this another one of your tests?"

"No, ma'am. Now would you take this? My arm is getting tired."

Gloria accepted the bottle but dared not open it.

"It would be a fun test though. Maybe I'll call it the 'Witcom Test,'" Dean Vickery said, twisting the top off another bottle. "Your sister confessed to what really happened."

"Oh my gosh. Is she . . . ?"

"She's going to be fine. She's in a detox unit and her children are with your mother. CPS is getting a no contact order filed until things get sorted out."

"What about my boys?"

"They're doing great. I think your mother can handle them for a little while longer. Now are you going to open that beer or let me drink alone?"

"You're pulling my leg."

"As long as you have known me, have I ever bluffed? Have I not always told the truth straight up?"

"Yes sir, you have. So, does this mean I am back at the academy now?"

"Gloria, you are free to walk right out that gate. Though I really hope you would enjoy a beer with me. Twist that top, girl."

Gloria twisted the top and took a long pull, savoring the alcoholic nectar of a well-brewed beer. She sank back in the seat and relaxed away her anxieties. "How did the rest of the class do?"

"All the drills have graduated here, except for one."

"Sorry sir, I did my best. I didn't want to let you down."

"Gloria, your charges are dropped. You're no longer a student; therefore you can't officially graduate someplace you never should have been."

"Who are you talking about?"

"Jamika Hawkins."

"Wow. I didn't expect that from her."

"The person she was to live with died and she didn't have a backup plan. So, I had to send her away."

"Holy cow. I never thought."

"She'll be okay though."

Gloria studied the dean. He had that rare glint in his eye, but she knew not to press him for details. She knew that he wouldn't say, and she wasn't one to pry.

"Ya know somethin,' Gloria?"

"What's that, sir?" she said after taking another pull off of the beer.

"You look horrible in orange. There's a box of your personal things in the barracks. Why don't you go check it out?"

Gloria stared at the dean for a long minute, evaluating the possibility and guarding herself against false hope. He waved her off.

Dean Vickery moved from the stool to his office chair after she disappeared inside. He smiled at the memories of seeing not a scared face but a determined one with a bit of uncertainty. He remembered watching her uncertainty quickly melt away as she dove into the program and helped her team become the first to graduate phase one.

He could see, even then, that her intelligence and demeanor did not match what her profile read. He knew that she was not the type of person to use drugs. All her toxicology tests came back negative, but she had been processed anyway. After finding out that her sister confessed to having the drugs in her car, he saw then the entire scheme of what the intent was.

He had put her file at the top of the pile, as he wanted to do what he could to get her back to her family as fast as possible. He instructed the counselors to coach her and give her free rein to complete the classes as fast as she could. It also helped that she had already taken many of the classes pertaining to business management in college. After having her first child, she had dropped out of school with only a semester to go. She never returned to school. Instead, she did her best to create a happy home until her husband walked out on her.

She soldiered on, keeping her boys in school and maintaining the house. Her mother helped tremendously while she worked two jobs, and her father floated her a bit extra when an unexpected expense came up.

The counselors had relayed all this information to him when it was time for the evaluations to be done. He wished she had had the courage to stand up for herself before. But if she had, they wouldn't have met, and she wouldn't have gained the strong independence that he now saw in her eyes.

Gloria came back out to join him. He handed back her beer. She took another sip and looked at him. "What happens now?" she asked, smoothing out her jeans and straightening her sweatshirt. Her feet soaked in the cushy comfort of her own well broken-in sneakers.

"Well, Miss Witcom, you are free to walk out that gate. I can call a cab for you and it will take you wherever you want to go. I presume home would be your destination." Dean Vickery took a swig from his beer, almost finishing it. "Or, you can climb that hill one more time. You know, just to tell it that it didn't beat you. Flip it off for the last time."

"Sir, no disrespect, but I would love to just go home."

"Gloria, I can only guess how you feel, but I think you'll thank me afterward." Gloria looked at him again. A sly, mischievous smile escaped his poker face. "Come on," he said and started out across the field.

Gloria caught up with him, stepping two of her short strides to his one. They stopped at the pile of boulders. She looked at the slings neatly laid out, ready for the next class to come in and start hauling boulders to the top of the hill only to have them slide back down on the cable and pulley.

"You lost track of how many times you carried one of these to the top, haven't you?"

"I couldn't begin to even guess, sir."

"You're still calling me sir?"

"Sorry, sir. I probably will until it fully sinks in that what you say is true."

238

"Well, I'll expect a Christmas card that is void of the reference to 'sir.'"

"Yes, sir. I can do that."

"You know you can't climb this hill without hauling a boulder up."

"Yes, sir. I know," Gloria said. Sipping the beer didn't feel like freedom. It was just a trivial thing that some people did. She imbibed periodically—usually only during bowling leagues—and she still limited herself to one. Most often she didn't even finish the one.

She noticed a stray boulder with a net slung around it lying haphazardly on the ground a few feet past a new concrete barrier.

Gripping her hands around the rough stone trickled the first sense of freedom into her spirit. The sensation of touching anything other than steel and concrete was exhilarating now, and the familiar feelings and textures triggered memories of building her confidence and self-esteem. After setting the boulder into the sling, she heaved it up on her shoulder. Her broken arm had healed well, and it felt strong as ever. She looked up the hill, preparing her mind for the climb.

"Okay, sir. I'll be back down in a bit."

"See you then."

Gloria had turned to leave when Dean Vickery stopped her again. "Gloria, there were a couple people dead set against your returning home."

"Sir?"

"I guess they are terribly concerned that you would dethrone them at the bowling alley when you return."

Gloria's eyes lit up as she watched a sincere smile spread across the dean's face. She found herself smiling also. Dean Vickery picked up her half-empty bottle of beer and started back toward the barracks.

"Before I forget . . ." Dean Vickery paused and turned again. Gloria turned back as well. "There was one person that has been near inconsolable until you stepped foot back onto this field. Fought for you tooth and nail. Biggest pain in my ass and the most impressive accomplishment. Made all the phone calls to everyone in your hometown, which I think inspired or maybe persuaded your sister to step forward."

"Sir." Gloria felt her throat start to choke down. "Who is it?"

"You'll find out soon." Dean Vickery turned and walked toward the barracks.

Chapter XXXIV

Gloria trudged up the last bit of steep hill, pausing to catch her breath as the beaten path began its gentler slope. It didn't seem like that long ago that she was easily packing one boulder after another up the monstrous hill. Now she wondered if a defibrillator was nearby.

Subtle changes like the blazing light that beat down on the top of the hill hinted at absenteeism. She remembered a nice shaded area as her memories flooded back but couldn't reason why it was different. The shed that allowed her to momentarily hide from the elements had a few new sheets of tin contrasting the older faded green ones. She knew something had changed but the exhaustion from the climb dulled her mind.

In no hurry, she tried to enjoy her last moments on this ground where she had learned so much about herself and taught so much to other young women who traversed this very trail. She wondered about Sarah and feared that as difficult as she had been, she surely would have been sent to prison. Sarah had fought her every step of the way. In the end, she knew that no matter where that young woman was, she was better for having divulged that secret. To be free of that horrific burden. She knew that the academy would see that she obtained proper counseling, even if she was sent back to prison.

Stepping casually around the brush, she listened to the birds chattering in the trees. A squirrel complained at her for passing too close—then a voice startled her out of her daydream.

"Are you having a problem with dust? I could get you a bucket of water."

Gloria looked to find the smiling face of her former assignment. Her heart was as light as a feather, seeing the troubled youth looking strong and confident. Sarah stood tall in a well-tailored pantsuit. Her standard-issue shoes were pristinely polished. Her hair was neatly wrapped into a bun. Her sleeves were cut just above the wrists to make them comfortable and to prevent entanglement in any office equipment. The shorter sleeves also offered a relief from the southern heat.

Gloria beamed and hurried to send the boulder down the zip line. It no longer felt heavy. It was just a minor annoyance that had to be dealt with, as a new, more pressing goal was a mere five seconds away. Gloria heaved the boulder up onto the cable and sent it hurling down to the bottom.

"Am I truly free?" Gloria asked.

"I have a copy of your papers right here."

"If I'm truly free, then I won't get in trouble for this." Gloria grabbed Sarah and pulled her into an embrace.

"You won't get in trouble. I might," Sarah said, wrapping her own arms around Gloria.

With an embrace that neither wanted to end, they finally broke apart, wiping stray tears from their cheeks.

Gloria looked at Sarah with the pride of a mother. Wiping a new flood of tears from her eyes, she held Sarah at arm's length to get a look at what a change she was witnessing. "You look amazing. Holy cow. New shoes, new suit, your hair done up neat and tight."

"This is just the first one. I'm supposed to check the fit and let the tailors know if there need to be any alterations. I asked to wear it today so I could look good for you," Sarah explained.

"Well, Miss Sarah, you look amazing. Not just the new clothes, but the attitude, the confidence and the strength of self. You are truly beautiful."

"I only got this far because of you. You made me feel that I was worth something. I wanted to show you that I am. I wanted to do this for you, so that you wouldn't be seen as a failure within the walls of the academy."

"What do you mean?" Gloria asked.

"I finished for you. I hauled all your remaining boulders up the hill, so you could graduate. I didn't care if *I* did, but as caring as you've been to me, I realized that I was a jerk and I needed my butt handed to me. I'm sorry I didn't tell you sooner. I'm sorry that I forced you to make that decision," Sarah said, choking down and losing her voice.

"Miss Sarah, I knew what I was doing. I prayed every night for an answer to get you to open up. The two nights before I was sent away—well I guess it was a few nights before that, because I didn't heed the answer for the last two or three days—I had a dream of paddling your backside. I felt in my bones that that was what I needed to do. I have never spanked my children. I never really had to and I swore that I never would. I always thought that if you start a child correctly, you won't ever have problems with discipline."

"I'm sorry. I don't think I was started correctly."

"You're fine. A lot of kids aren't disciplined properly. A stern look for some will set them straight, where others are like knot-headed mules. Got to give them a swat to get their attention."

Sarah smiled as she recognized the ever-vigilant mom coming through to teach yet another lesson.

"Yes, mom," Sarah said in an exasperated teenager tone.

"How's your studies going?" Gloria asked as Sarah guided them to sit under the lean-to.

"They're going well. I'm keeping pace with everyone. A little slow in language arts but I'm still getting it."

"What's your goals afterward?"

"Oh geez. Everyone asks me this. I studied so many laws, looking for loopholes, writing letters to lawyers, studying how the court systems work and the requirements needed when asking for a pardon."

"You asked for a pardon, for me?"

"Yes, ma'am. I called everyone in your hometown asking if they would write a letter to the governor asking for you to be pardoned. I sited the average for a first-time offense was well below what you had served. And your sister came to the state capitol to personally hand him her letter confessing that she didn't have a spine—she begged to switch places with you because she was to blame."

"Wow. You really went to bat for me," Gloria said as a proud mother's smile spread across her face.

Sarah smiled, also proud that she had accomplished what she had set out to do. It had been a monumental task and she wanted to give up numerous times, but she saw it through, and the reward was oh, so sweet. She now understood the Japanese proverb, "Life without endeavor is like entering a jewel mine and coming out with empty hands."

"You did the same for me, Miss Gloria." Sarah smiled back at her mentor. "I have something for you." Sarah flipped open the folder she held and drew out a small packet of papers.

244

"This is your pardon—or a copy of it." She handed the papers to Gloria.

Gloria took the papers and scanned them, looking for anything that was recognizable. Tears battled to escape from her eyes and eventually won, creating twin rivers flowing down her cheeks. Her fingers traced over the governor's signature and a shadow of the raised impression of the state seal.

"You gave me the very thing I needed to set me free," Sarah said. "I had to do the same for you. I had to see that you made it home to your sons. A life without you as their mother is no life at all."

Gloria pulled her into another hug as she fought back the sobs that screamed to be let out.

"Come on. Walk with me, please?" Sarah turned toward the back gate. "Dean Vickery said that you couldn't be an actual graduate from the academy, since you've been pardoned, which kinda voids your time. He said that the pardon is likely temporary since they have lawyers working on getting your charges dropped completely. But you may have to go back before the judge for perjury."

A young woman in a blue drill uniform stood by the gate, waiting for their approach. She pulled out her keys and opened the lock on the gate. Pulling it open, she followed them through.

"So, you're doing well now?" Gloria asked, still concerned for Sarah's well-being.

"Yes, ma'am. I will be interning for Walstein, Morgan and Cole soon while I finish my classes here. I know it will be tough but I know that I can manage. I'm learning so many new things about myself and society as a whole, without getting in trouble. I don't think I would have ever been able to excel this far on my own. It's hard, but I can see that it's worth every sore muscle and headache."

"Wow. Well, I definitely feel a bit underdressed compared to you," Gloria said as she followed Sarah on the narrow path. "You never told me what you wanted to do after your schooling."

"I thought I would go into law. I've seen both sides of the fence. I think I can help in some aspect. I hope my internship goes well and I get a good recommendation into law school. I thought I would apply after I get my bachelor's. I think it's kinda fascinating, in a way."

"By the book, by the number," Gloria said, having to sidestep around a fallen tree. "Be harsh in your convictions, be balanced in your sentence suggestions. Regardless, I'm so proud of everything you're doing and everything you've accomplished."

"Thank you. You know, that's the first time someone has ever said that to me."

Gloria studied her for a moment. "I think you're going to hear it a lot more often."

Sarah grinned as they stepped to the side of the platform where the locked box held multiple harnesses for the zip line. Sarah helped Gloria into a harness, then they stepped up on the platform and looked down on the crowd gathered around the gate at the end of the zip line. The crowd held their distance except for three individuals who stood just a few feet from where their mother would greet them.

"Those are my boys!" Gloria called out excitedly. "Oh my gosh. Dean Vickery really wasn't pulling my leg."

Gloria and Sarah looked at the compound below and the throng of people waiting at the end of the zip line. Gloria waved at the gathering crowd. She heard a cheer go up at the wave. Canopies covered several tables to shield guests from the sun while smoke lifted into the air from the academy's mobile kitchen.

"Dean Vickery had them drive out yesterday. He instructed me to give you your pardon at the top of the hill and walk with you back here. He's been planning this ever since I traded a crab dinner for a five-minute audience with Governor Reynolds."

"You traded a crab dinner for my pardon?"

"Yeah. That's a story for another time, but it was worth the trade." Sarah smiled at her mentor, barely able to contain her joy at seeing this woman fly home.

"It was the dean's idea to make you an honorary graduate. He said that you had worked too hard not to enjoy at least some of the perks of graduating."

"I'll settle for anywhere my feet stay on the ground." Gloria voiced her concern over her nearly paralyzing fear of heights.

The drill in blue fatigues strapped a helmet on her, then cinched up her harness to make sure she wasn't going to fall out of it. Sarah grinned at the woman she had thought was as fearless as a mama bear. She realized now that even this mama bear had boundaries—ones she knew she would cross if the reason was compelling enough.

The drill stepped to the edge of the platform and opened the safety gate. A bead of sweat formed on Gloria's brow. The day was hot, yet Sarah figured that Gloria's anxiety doubled the stream that had already started trickling down her face.

"Can I just walk around and come up the drive?" Gloria's anxiety was spiking to a perilous dose.

"Come on, mama bear. This is the fastest way to get to your boys," Sarah chided. "What kind of example are you setting for your sons by chickening out of a little zip line?"

Gloria beamed a glare to Sarah as she prepared herself for launch. She had survived this once before when she graduated phase one. Now she was supposed to be free to make her own decisions. So how could she be forced to do this—something that she was terrified of?

Gloria hesitated, afraid to let go of the railing. Her anxiety caused her to tighten her grip on the handrail.

"Mom."

Gloria turned at the all-too-familiar title.

"Will you adopt me?"

Gloria stared at Sarah, trying to understand the reason for such a question.

"I need a mother strong enough to put me in my place. I want you to be that mom."

Gloria's expression remained blank as she sought to assemble the dots of Sarah's life. She hadn't remotely thought that that was what Sarah needed in her life. Now she knew what Sarah needed. She needed someone to side with her all those years ago. Someone to teach her empathy, respect and real—to the core—love.

"Finish strong and we'll talk about it," Gloria said with a mischievous glint in her eye.

"Just like you?" Sarah asked.

Gloria glanced up at the carabiner, looking for any defect that would give her an excuse to bow out of the flight to freedom. The handrail on one side gave her little comfort in keeping her safe on the platform when the opening to her freedom had a drop of dozens of feet to the undergrowth below.

Gloria picked her feet up off the platform and turned loose of the handrail. "Just like me," she called out as she slowly gained momentum, sailing down the steel cable toward her three boys and a wide-open gate to freedom.

Hello again my friends,

Thank you for staying with me through the second book in this trilogy. I believe that this one will have been the hardest to write. At the moment, I am halfway finished writing *The Diploma* and know where the characters will be at the conclusion of the trilogy.

My parents may not admit it, but I was the difficult child growing up. Getting into fights, getting bad grades, not doing what I was told, you know the type. Somehow—I made it through adolescence and into adulthood where the lessons were fewer, but tougher. I made many bad choices, but still didn't care to actually learn until one seemingly correct choice caused the choice of another. Sorry, I'm not going to elaborate on this until maybe an autobiography years down the road.

The result changed me. I no longer sought what is out there for me; instead I began to think about the most dreaded word on an exam—Why? *Why* is the most dreaded word to me and maybe to you as well, but I found that it is the most important word. It's important because it requires thought. Thought, by its nature, requires reason. The reason you do something can *make* you or *break* you.

A decision to develop a craft of stealing could very well *break* you and land you a lengthy sentence. But, if turned around, it could *make* you by allowing you to get paid to show others how they are vulnerable and to show them how to protect themselves and their property.

In *The Scholarship*, I described the tools you need to live a full and productive life. But, tools aren't any good if you don't have a goal to apply them toward and thus a reason to make your goal worthwhile. If you could jump straight to the finish line by stacking the deck like my little sister did when playing Candyland, you'd miss out on all the struggles that build you as a person along the way.

When you struggle with something, it is a lesson in the making. You slip on a patch of ice, you get a lesson on where not to step. You see a friend slip on a patch of ice, you advance your gingerbread man around the danger. That's your small win for the day. This awareness is your classroom. Watching how things unfold and weighing the pros and cons of your decisions.

This is what our journey is about. Of course it's about entertainment, but it's also about becoming a better part of our community by being aware of the interconnected relationships that we all have with people around the world. This world is our classroom, our teacher and our student. We are all, at least in part, dependent on each other to become the best person we can be for ourselves and for others.

Thank you for reading, and I can't wait to hear from you.

Alex R Price
P.O. Box 593
Green River, WY 82935

alex@alexrpriceauthor.com
alexrpriceauthor.com